The Kidnapped:

A Collection of Short Stories

Dwight L. Wilson

This is a work of historical fiction. Names, characters, places, and incidents are primarily based on true historic figures.

Text copyright © 2018 Running Wild Press

Cover image copyright © 2018 Dan Fernandez

Published in the United States by Running Wild Press.
Visit Running Wild Press on the web at www.runningwildpress.com
Educators, librarians, book clubs (as well as the eternally curious), go to
www.runningwildpress.com for teaching tools.

ISBN 9781947041073 (pbk)
ISBN 9781947041080 (eBook)

Library of Congress Control Number: 2017962963

Printed in the United States of America.

AUTHOR'S NOTE

The author spent more than a dozen years researching the time period and geographical areas into which these stories are placed. This is a work of fiction peopled by many real characters, most of whom play cameos, and some of whom are the author's relatives. None of the dialogue is actual and a few events created. Nearly all of the situations were possible.

1737 — All the Light
1814/1795 — From Africa
1825 — One of the Few
1827 — Freedom Seekers
1829 — Northern Dreams
1831 — Allies
1832 — Impatient Patience
1832 — Kentucky Drums
1832 — Mountain Climbing
1832 — Who Are We
1842 — Freedom Day
1846 — Spring
1846 — Possibilities
1847 — Freedom Seeds
1856 — Credentials

MAIN CHARACTERS IN *KIDNAPPED*

HOUSE OF ESI

Esi — Fante Matriarch enslaved at age 12 in 1795

Kofi (AKA Kenneth) — Esi's Fante Husband enslaved at age 12 in 1795

*Sarah — Esi's youngest daughter and narrator, author's 4th Great
 Grandmother

Fannie — Esi's 3rd daughter

Marshall Lucky — Fannie's 2nd husband, a trapper

Sally — Fannie's niece/adopted daughter whose parents were Dan
 and Val

Charlotte — Esi's oldest child

*Robin — Esi's 2nd child,1st son

Dan Crispin — Esi's 3rd child, 2nd son

Luther — Esi's 4th son

Diego Perez — Dan's 1st son

Zephyrine — Dan's wife

HOUSE OF CAESAR

*Caesar I — Born in 1712, Kimbundu enslaved by Aaron Prescott

Tilly — Wife of Caesar I

*Caesar IV — Born in 1792, African-Shawnee warrior

Monni — Monacan wife of Caesar IV

PATIENCE STARBUCK FAMILY

Patience Starbuck — Born in 1798, Wealthy Quaker Abolitionist and feminist

Thomas Hussey — Born 1788, Patience's husband

Emma Bernard Folger — Born in1826, Patience's niece and Thomas's 2nd wife

PRESCOTT FAMILY

Aaron Prescott — Born in 1710 Quaker slave holder of Caesar I and Tilly

Ellen Prescott — Born in 1711 Quaker slave holder of Caesar I and Tilly

Nathan Prescott — Born in 1786, great grandson of Aaron and Ellen

FERGUSON FAMILY

*Mary Crispin Ferguson — Born in 1785, author's Quaker 5th great grandmother

*Clark Ferguson — Born in 1786, author's Quaker 5th great grandfather

*Charles Ferguson — Born in 1814, author's Quaker 4th great grandfather

*Elizabeth Ferguson — Born in 1810, daughter of Mary Crispin and Clark

OTHER NOTABLE CHARACTERS

Val Lucky — Fannie's best friend

*Angelina Grimké — Quaker abolitionist and feminist

*Sarah Grimké — Quaker abolitionist and feminist

*Sarah Mapps Douglass — Quaker abolitionist and educator

*Harriet Beecher Stowe — Abolitionist and writer

Margery Lloyd Barclay — British Quaker

*Lucy Stone — Abolitionist and feminist

*John Fairchild — Kentucky abolitionist

Naphtali Long — Black slave catcher

Autumn Turtle — Shawnee seer

Gray Eyed Cougar — Bannock war chief

Swift Eagle — Bannock warrior

Nellie/Nana — Black freedwoman

*Tiana Rogers — Cherokee wife of Sam Houston

*Sam Houston — Former governor of Tennessee

*Robert Matson — Kentucky/Illinois slave master

* Historical Figures

INTRODUCTION

My name is Sarah Ferguson. I was born in slavery but, with the help of the Underground Railroad, stole myself and fled to Ohio.

Today, December 2, 1859, John Brown will be hanged in Harper's Ferry. A few of my relatives were with him. Others were en route when his rebellion began earlier than planned. Throughout this torn land colored folk are crying over the injustice of this hero's impending death. There can be no better time than now to begin this long-delayed narrative. The "Old Man" chose to live his life to prevent a multitude of the stories that I shall share from being repeated.

Blood is overrated. The only functional kinship is personal engagement that empowers or destroys potential. I have kept a journal since age ten, but in composing this collection I needed collaborators. The first is my sister Fannie who listened to the stories of our mother when I was busy closing my ears to Africa, choosing instead to focus on the America I hoped to see. It took Mama's loss for me to take the whole world seriously. As a child I was ashamed of many parts of this woman. Now I am a woman who accepts all of her, the great one named Esi.

Our extended family includes Caesar IV, great grandson of the first Caesar who in 1737 was rescued by the Shawnees and his Monacan wife Monni. These Native Americans are joined in "The House of Esi" by the wealthy, risk-taking, Quaker abolitionist, Patience Starbuck.

Each story is fundamental to the building of America. They speak to the kidnapping of humans, their land or their ability to dream and the privilege afforded to those with whiteness or wealth and especially a combination of both. Each of the privileged is not an oppressive actor. Each of those of color is not heroic. Survivors, not victims are the foci. Regardless of circumstances, optimism fuels decisions.

ALL THE LIGHT

Around campfires and with trusted friends who worked the Underground Railroad with him, my friend Caesar, the fourth in his line to wear this name, used the following as his foundation story. Perhaps I heard it as many times as the Hebrews heard about their escape from Egypt. With minimal embellishments, I retell it.

The Quaker, Aaron Prescott, came to Virginia to do good and was doing quite well. By 1730 he owned 400 acres and 22 slaves. Daily visions of more land worked by more slaves danced in his head. Among the skilled laborers under his direction was a blacksmith named Caesar and his wife Tilly. Neither had a surname, for as Aaron explained to his wife, Ellen, "To afford darkies surnames, especially if it were *our* name, might mislead people into thinking my blood has been mixed with theirs. Such an abomination would cast a shadow on God."

In an attempt to maintain his own purity, Prescott's plan of ownership was a careful one. He would only purchase couples able to reproduce free property, treat them better than did neighbor slaveholders, never sell slaves or land. When times were good, buy more of both.

"If thee keeps thy word," said Ellen, "thee will be seen as a paragon of virtue."

"I am a Friend. More than that, I am a Prescott. My word is as good as the day is long."

He had an edge to his tone. Since she was only observing, not trying to challenge her husband, Ellen said no more.

The claim that he was still a member of the Religious Society of Friends was a stretch. An elder had caught Aaron and Ellen in a compromising position a few weeks before their wedding. A hastily called meeting of the overseers had led to both being disowned from the local meeting's membership rolls. Following a civil wedding which Quakers considered uncivilized, they had boldly continued to attend meeting for worship.

◊◊◊◊◊◊

In 1737 Caesar and Tilly counted many blessings. First among them was the fact that both came from Kimbundu families who had arrived in America in 1619 and whose mothers had kept the first tongue alive. They had no way of prophesying that one day their descendants would not only fight with Tecumseh, a visionary Shawnee who would lead one of the greatest Native American confederacies, but also become legendary abolitionists.

Caesar saw his wife combing the grass as she came toward his blacksmith shop. "What are you studying, dear one?" He said in Kimbundu.

"Four leaf clovers; they are good luck."

"Who told you that lie? Three or four leafs; what does it matter?"

"I heard it from a woman when we were serving the masters the meal following meeting for worship."

"Now four leaf clovers are added to looking for comets?" he said with the sweet smile reserved for the woman he loved.

"Are we not lucky? There are slaves nearby who have been beaten within a finger's width of their lives, and your friend Cuffee had his big toes cut off when he was caught trying to escape."

"But—"

Before he could finish the argument, Prescott suddenly emerged from around the shop's corner. "How many times must I say no foreign languages? Another master would sell one or both!"

"Yessir, Master," said Caesar bowing.

"And thee, Tilly, why is thee dilly dallying from thy work?"

"Master Aaron, sir, I just bringing my husband the noon meal."

"I see nothing but grass in thy hand."

"I musta just forgot it." She appeared flustered as she sprinted back to the house.

"In some matters thee and thy wife are beyond stupid," said Prescott. "Take away thy ability with metals and Tilly's with midwifing, and you would be worthless. Doesn't thee agree?"

Caesar simply looked on as though he were too dumb to understand so deep a question. Prescott spun away to check on the men and women in the fields.

He was out of sight when Tilly returned with a piece of fatback and a hunk of cornbread.

"How did you forget my food?" said Caesar in Kimbundu.

"I do not remember the last time I forgot something. I was only coming out to see how you are doing and to steal a kiss."

He gave her a long kiss before accepting the food.

"Now I must carry supper to the field hands. It wasn't quite ready."

◊◊◊◊◊◊

Magnanimously, Prescott worked with his slaves, at least 'work' is what he called it. Behind his back, his field hands referred to his efforts as, "*Playing* at work." His belief in modeling the equality of all stopped when it came to eating the midday and late meals. Those he took with his wife, lying to himself that the sole reason for doing so was because, "We are a family."

He entered his dining room and was happy to see that instead of fatback and cornbread, his table held pork roast, potatoes, field greens, spoonbread, and buttermilk.

"Thee does make the best buttermilk," he said to Tilly before she disappeared to the backroom to eat her slave fare.

Ellen puckered up for a kiss. He gave her a light smooch, patted his four year old son on the head and said, "Thomas, soon thee will have a little brother or sister."

"Yes he will," said Ellen. "The best purchase thee ever made was Tilly as a midwife cook and Caesar as a blacksmith and carpenter."

"The two of those scoundrels cost me enough."

"Scoundrels?" she said surprised at his words. "I lost four straight babies before she successfully delivered Thomas, and nothing is broken long with Caesar around."

"It is not their work that concerns me. It is their sneaky shiftlessness. I caught them speaking African again."

"The language is Kimbuda," said Ellen, butchering the word.

"It is of Africa, and it as forbidden as drums and their superstitious gods. They take advantage of our kindness, Ellen. Just once I should send them to the gaol for a good beating."

"No!"

"It would not have to be 40 lashes. I'm sure 20 would beat the Africa out of them."

◊◊◊◊◊◊

That night, in bed, Tilly reported the conversation and more. "I overheard Master Aaron say his creditors are pressing him for money."

"What do you think he will do?"

"I have no idea, but he told Ellen he will not sell land under any circumstances."

"Not even the lower 80 acres he bought last year and he is keeping fallow?"

"No."

"What is left to sell?" said Tilly.

◊◊◊◊◊◊

Tears fell while Prescott prepared for his first slave sale. Earlier in the day he had drawn lots from the field hands. One child each was sold from five families. The cries from the oppressed put his tears to shame, but his 480 acres remained intact.

Tilly said to Caesar, "The Prescotts felt they were doing us a favor by keeping our son's name out of the hat."

"They were," said Caesar.

"How can it be a favor to make us marked? Directing their rage at the Prescotts would be futile, so our people are mean to us instead."

"As long as James remains with us, who cares?"

Prescott had sold the minimum number of children to stay afloat. When business did not improve, and the next creditor stepped forward, he upped the ante.

With all of the parents of slave children assembled, he said, "I am sad to say that I have no choice but to draw lots again."

"Sir," said a woman who had already lost a child in the first sale, "will us that already give up a baby have to be in that hat again?"

Prescott was a fair man. However, to maintain his own ease he said, "This is a new day. Every family who has at least one remaining child will have to be entered in the lottery. That includes the two of you three who still counts more than one child as well as *all* families who have not lost a single child."

All eyes turned to Caesar and Tilly. Which of them reached first for the other's hand will never be known. What is known is that day James was lost forever to his parents.

Tilly fell to her knees sobbing, "Master, please don't take my onliest child. I done brought to birth two for you; ain't that worth something?"

7

"Stand, dear," said Caesar in Kimbundu, defiantly breaking the no foreign language rule. "Please stand."

Prescott overlooked the violation. As Caesar helped Tilly find her legs, Prescott said, "Fair is fair. This hurts me more than it hurts you. The eight families whose straws were drawn should have a child in the barn waiting for the dealer by dawn the day after tomorrow."

Prescott returned to the big house on the little hill. Ellen knew that he had just conducted the lottery. Trying to shield the sordid affair from her mind, while rocking the newborn with one hand, she kept her eyes on the letter she held in the other.

Aaron said, "I just had one of the worst days of my life, and thee acts as though thee is wedded to a piece of paper!"

Ellen folded the letter. "This is a pamphlet sent by my Aunt Phoebe of New Jersey. It was written by Friend John Hepburn in 1715 and is called, 'Arguments Against Making Slaves of Men'; he is clear that we are wrong to hold others in bondage. Should we not free all of the slaves we hold instead of selling them piecemeal?"

"Thee is acting as foolish as Tilly. How can I free our slaves and force our family to live destitute? Would thee have me go to the poor house?"

"But Hepburn believes we are sinning, and when I read his words to Tilly she said the same."

The usually mild-mannered Aaron slammed his beaver hat on the table. "I was warned not to marry thee. Now I have a wife taking counsel from a slave!"

He stormed out of the room.

From her place at the stove, Tilly had heard every word but would not be able to make a report to Caesar until their work day ended. They had more important matters to discuss than Aaron's anger.

◊◊◊◊◊◊

Caesar was in the hut they shared with another couple when Tilly arrived. The near neighbors were among the first families to lose a child. The mother gave Tilly a smug look which she ignored. The four slaves made small talk about the weather before retiring to their separate corners. Once beneath the thin blanket Tilly whispered, "Did you tell James?"

"You can speak as loud as you want. Those two do not know our language."

"James does," said Tilly before releasing the tears she had hidden in the big house. She cried so hard that, in Caesar's embrace, together they shook as though the earth were quaking. When she was able to speak she said, "What are we going to do? I have helped Ellen have two children, but it is as though she has stolen my luck. I have not been pregnant since we came here, and now—"

"Shh, my dear," he interrupted, "you'll wake James."

"He will know soon enough, will he not?"

Each slept fitfully. Before dawn, Caesar woke James and led him outside the hut. When he stopped and searched for the words he had composed mentally during the night James said, "I already know, Daddy. I am being sent away like the other children were."

"Are you not afraid?"

"Yes, I am afraid; but I am a warrior, and now people will not stare at me with hatred because I was saved when their children were not."

James returned to the hut where he calmly ate his porridge before going to the vegetable gardens to pull weeds with the others in his age set. His father was speechless.

◊◊◊◊◊◊

Prescott had gone to bed seething. In the morning Tilly awakened him with a knock and a respectful pause before delivering his toast, eggs, and coffee in bed. "Thee stepped over the line yesterday, Tilly."

"How so, Master?" she said trembling.

"Thee called my wife—and me for that matter—sinners."

"I didn't mean to offend nobody," she said head bowed and tried to ease out the door.

"Stand still, girl!" he said. "When I sell the children tomorrow, thee too will be sold. Dismissed." She stood her ground. "Thee defies me in my presence?"

"I ain't trying to defy, but I gotta ask, I mean beg, a favor." He did not stop her. "If you done made up yo' mind to do this evil, can you at least sell me with my boy?" While he was thinking over the question she added, "You used to talk 'bout not breaking up families."

"Get out of my sight." He pointed towards the door.

When the slave merchant visited, the good Quaker offered up eight children and one woman. Prescott also requested the slave Tilly and son go to the same buyer.

"I can't make promises about merchandise," said the slave merchant, "but I will attempt to keep them together. In fact, if it is within $25 of the offering price, I will do my Christian best to sell the niggers as one."

"I cannot ask for more."

◊◊◊◊◊◊

The slaves had heard that the Shawnees raided throughout Northern Virginia. Most were afraid of warriors called heathens. Aaron boasted to an assembly of slaves, "They never hurt Quakers. They know that we are a peaceful people who never resort to violence."

Caesar prayed that the Prescotts would be the exception.

Indeed a few of their neighbors dressed in Quaker garb as a way to protect themselves. Of course, if given the opportunity, these same neighbors would happily blow off a Shawnee's head.

A raiding party showed up on the Prescott plantation. Although they did not hurt the only white man on the property or any of the slaves, they stripped the big house of everything they thought was valuable. The Shawnees were about to leave for the next plantation when Caesar called out and came to the leader.

"I'd like to go with you men," he said.

The interpreter was a white man adopted into the tribe. He explained the black man's words.

The Shawnee leader of the war party said something incomprehensible. The interpreter turned back to Caesar and said, "You're welcome to join us."

Initially startled, Prescott found his voice, "This is thy home, Caesar. Would thee leave me for these heathens? Up until the last month, when *I had no choice*, thee hast been my brother and I thy keeper."

Caesar had less respect for the Quakers he knew than he did the Shawnees. He was tempted to grab a tool and shove it down Aaron's throat. Instead he said, "You sold my son. Then you sold my wife. Now you want to keep me? Find yourself a new fool."

FROM AFRICA

My mother, Esi, granddaughter of a Fante Queen Mother enjoyed telling of the births of each of her children. For this tale I am beholden to both repeated hearings and the edits of my older sister, Fannie.

The summer day in 1814 dawned cloudless. Mama lay on a thin blanket spread on a dirt floor, dreaming of Fante-land where her bed would have been made by artisans employed by the Queen Mother. Her small slave shack held a single chair and straw mats with the family's few extra pieces of clothing folded neatly in a corner. Already the August heat was stifling. Spread around the shack were gourds of soap suds covered with slices of bread whose undersides were coated with molasses. The bread had holes in their center that were an inviting trap. These temptations were designed by Daddy, a man who did everything within his power to protect his family's comfort. Fat flies flew above those that had been lured inside. Mama was oblivious both to the flies and the hordes of buzzing mosquitoes. Praying both for Daddy and me, her unborn child, she was deep inside an act of love, forcing all her energy to be positive. I had begun my descent a few hours after midnight. Immediately Daddy left to request the midwife come running. He would be barred from the hut until after the birth.

At this moment Mama's contention was less with childbirth and more with her fascination with memory. Amidst the womb's new set of clenching and releasing, Mama once more coveted retractions. How had Anansi, the Trickster God, allowed their capture and the downward spiral that it had set off? Why wouldn't he, or couldn't he, reverse his decisions?

"In search of Fante-land," according to Mama, I peered through human leather; skin once smooth and glossy with palm oil was divinely lined from other births and spitefully lined from a bevy of beatings delivered by whip lashes ostensibly directed at her back that had enwrapped her entire torso. The lines were drawn by her first master for such offenses as overcooking a pudding, picking a few pounds of Sea Island cotton less than her daily quota, and having the temerity to forget that an eight- year-old white child should be addressed as "sir."

As she did with each of her births, Mama prayed for my safe arrival. She breathed deeply and once more sang the Fante soothing-song her mother had taught her:

"Oh my sweet one,
the sun is your friend.
Watch the cassava leaf
reach toward sky.
Remember your ancestors
and why they still live.

"Oh my sweet one,
the sun is your friend.
Watch the violets
reach toward sky.
Remember your siblings
and why…"

I had heard the song so often that I thought it was my song. It was almost as familiar as her heart beat. I pushed again, and Mama's singing was interrupted by the contraction. When release came, Esi found herself in the year 1795, a twelve-year-old, back in Fante-land. Lost, lonely, and wanting for the first time in years to hold her mother's hand, Esi was shoved with the other children to the rear of the line. A few spaces behind her in line was Kofi, who one day would be her husband. At twelve, there in the sheltering fine greenery, none of the kidnapped thought of a future. Years later they would be told they had no history.

The trip through the rain forest was surreal. The captives sang sorrow songs that are still being shaped. The lyrics admitted defeat but made clear their intention to rally. Even while singing along, or listening to newly improvised phrases, initially Esi enjoyed the vitality in the merging of a million vibrant scents as well as the shapes and myriad colors of trees and grasses. Prior to her kidnapping, she had taken most aesthetics for granted. Now no two creations were alike. No one was to be forgotten. Each piece of greenery seemed to desire her touch, but even the closest ones were out of reach unless the line leaned one way or her captors forced her to go another. Here in chains, she was almost dizzy from life's denied possibilities.

"Be strong," she heard Kofi whisper, as much to himself as to her.

Single file, the line entered through a narrow gate. Without ceremony, horror struck as all the children under age ten, including her sister Adwoa, were stripped away. They would never survive what was to come. Next the men were separated from the women and shunted under guard off to a separate room. Kofi's eyes followed Esi as much as his recently widowed mother. A sudden blow from a whip redirected his eyes to the back of the man behind the man in front. The last of the kidnapped entered the stone edifice. The iron gate clanged shut and was locked by two armed guards. For most of the captured, this would be the last time friends and relatives would see each other: they slipped into a white-made darkness, losing their place in circles that were centuries old. Mama said that if she had known her fate on that day she might have given up hope. Her ignorance fueled our lives.

Twice a day, silent workers made their way among the chained kidnapped. Theirs was a vain attempt to mask stench from spilled blood, body waste, and vomit so rank it made eyes water. They took pride in their work because they had nothing else, and these were their people. In this darkened, stifling space, they would ply their unpaid occupation until health failed them: locked in a dungeon devoid of hope, mopping the residue of despair.

The kidnapped were warehoused on what slavers called "The Gold Coast" in reference to both the precious ore and blacks who enriched the pockets of others in search of their bounty. More captives joined daily. After a month of waiting, the time came to depart. Led by a sailor carrying a whale oil lamp, the slaves shuffled down steps, fearing certain beatings and possible broken bones. They held each other with cuffed hands to prevent tripping. They were ordered to lie down on wooden benches in a room whose ceiling was so close that, on her back, Esi could touch it without extending her arm more than a foot above her nose. She blinked in terror. The ceiling seemed to be lowering. Someone behind her screamed, and another prayed for mercy. Esi thought she was at the end of the line, but a whip butt prodded her to move closer to the neighbor in front. She inched forward and rolled to her side. The chains tightened and she felt the pressed breasts of the girl behind her. Esi inhaled, hoping to avoid touching her other neighbor's rear. She exhaled, and a minute later the death-colored man forced a new body into the pack. Esi felt panting breath on her back. She said a prayer, first for the terrified girl behind her and then for herself. Soon it seemed that everyone on the bench was systematically linked closer than the intertwined circles of any man-made chain. Before journey's end, she would conclude that they had been transformed into a single tribe. Never again would she think in terms of tribes or ethnicities. Black was black.

A tobacco-laden rain of spit fell from the upper deck. The sailors above, most of whom probably had been pressed onto the slave ship, tried to convince everyone that those below were inhuman monstrosities.

"Oh, Nyame," Esi prayed, "teach me to survive. Let me withstand all that might dishonor the ancestors, limit my descendants."

The ship cast off. Hours later a handful of slaves were directed to troughs of food filled with a concoction of palm oil, water, corn, peppers, horse beans, rice, salt and yams. For the next sixty days, with the exception of Sundays, twice a day, from the never-washed tub, this would be her regular meal. The exception was Sundays which the enslavers said was "dedicated to the Lord." Then the slaves would be fed rice, beans, and small scraps from the boiled heads of smoked swine. On the ship's deck Esi looked up and saw Kofi's eyes smiling at her. "Don't worry; I'm here." Although he could not understand the language, a sailor cuffed him in the ear and kicked him in the side. Embarrassed, Kofi looked away. What could a twelve-year-old do to protect her in this place?

Esi was sleeping when she was awakened by slow steady drips. She screamed, thinking it was a repeat of the spitting and tried to dodge, but she did not have sufficient range of motion to remove her whole body. She remembered her mother's teachings about mental fortitude and calmed down. Upon returning to her original position she realized the drops were water. She counted them to 98 and fell asleep.

There were losses on the journey despite the efforts of the guards and a doctor employed primarily to keep alive the cargo. Among the fatalities were women who drowned themselves either resisting or after being raped and men killed in a failed rebellion. Others died of the measles, flu, and dysentery, or were thrown overboard while still alive. Epidemics jeopardized everyone. Babies and mothers died during childbirth. A pact of five men threw themselves overboard. The terrorized assumed on such a journey, all of this was commonplace in this new world. Mama would never credit herself with being one who had chosen to survive, because she never remembered why she had made the choice. Daddy once said, "If the Atlantic dried like the Red Sea, one could use bones to trace back to Africa. It won't, so let's be content with America."

◊◊◊◊◊◊

My parents came to America as property intended to make the country great. They both knew this, but deep differences existed between their reactions to this unfortunate fundamental truth. Mama refused to abandon her Fante ways, clinging to the firm belief that someday she would go home, while Daddy now called himself Kenneth and focused on assimilating. Mama heard the word Christian and searched, but by their Bible's standard, she was unable to find a single white one. She refused to stop praying to Nyame, while Daddy swore that Jehovah sat on the new world's throne, and was thus the only true American deity. Mama believed that sexual relations could only be meaningful between equals; Daddy cringed every time she was touched by the master or eyeballed by the overseer. Mama reveled in misspeaking English; because the bored master wanted Daddy as a study partner, he enabled Daddy to have the ability to speak English with earls and Latin with professors. All the easily touched differences were measured by outsiders, but my parents believed that love and devotion covered all gaps, healed all wounds, and cleansed all evils.

◊◊◊◊◊◊

Babies are not known for eternal patience. The last contraction ended, and Ama, the mute midwife motioned for the final push. "Brown baby," Mama said. "Beautiful brown baby. Master's beautiful brown baby."

Which came first, life or love? Nathan Prescott, descendant of Quakers, would never claim a brown child as his flesh, but love prevented Mama from hating me. Kofi had accepted each of Esi's five older babies that had thus far survived their passage into Virginia. Not all of us were his direct descendants, but Kofi was my daddy. He had enough to overcome in knowing that whenever Master chose to call, he was moved either into the bachelors' cabin or into the field. Where he slept on those nights depended upon the amount of fortitude he summoned. All my life at Fruits of the Spirit Plantation, I loved my daddy because he developed inner fortitude to sustain a love that never went out of season.

Mama smiled at me as I suckled. Her smile was solely in hope that she could instill the glitter that she believed she herself had lost on the day of her captivity. Once in a while, she admitted freedom could not have been as sweet as memory. She knew slavery tinted everything in its path ripe apple red. Squinting through the dim morning light, Mama thought that my closed eyes meant I was beyond influence. She glanced up at Ama whose hand gesture made it clear that in the mother's milk was tomorrow's promise. Esi smiled again at me. Bitterness receded with love's advance.

◊◊◊◊◊◊

Daddy was met at the door of the slave cabin by the oldest surviving child, eight-year-old Charlotte. She already worked in the vegetable fields where Mama was forewoman after originally being cook.

Daddy was anxious to attend to his wife and meet me. But nothing could have made him overlook a child's welcome. He stopped and offered a hand to Charlotte, "Congratulations, daughter. It is my understanding you have been blessed with a new sister."

"Sho' 'nuff," said Charlotte as she held herself back from seeking the kiss she would have preferred. Daddy looked at her sternly. "Sure enough, sir," she corrected herself. "I didn't mean to speak wrong."

"Remember, Charlotte," said Daddy, "you are the first, and you must lead the others."

My older brothers ran up next. They too received a congratulatory handshake plus a pat on the head. To make them hard for a cruel world, once it was decided that they understood right from wrong, they were never embraced. The boys merely fell in behind Daddy. To their surprise, Daddy did not follow his practice of first playing with his children and then embracing Mama. He went straight to where his wife lay exhausted on their straw pallet. Daddy fell on his knees with his head ever so slightly bowed. For her ordeal or should-be position? We never asked. Mama waited for him with a smile. His fatigue retreated in her glow. "How you be, Kofi?"

"Sweet Esi, darling," he whispered, "I've worried about you all day." He kissed her brow.

"I loves you," said Mama loud enough for all her children to hear the indisputable truth.

He lay down next to Mama. "Take your rest, Esi. I will protect you. I am home now."

◊◊◊◊◊◊

Mama was happy to be in her lover's arms, but each time Mama repeated my birthday story—or that of any of her other children—whether or not Daddy was present, she was careful to remind listeners that we were Fante and America could not be our homeland. She drifted off to sleep. Upon awaking, Mama found Daddy holding me, and I was whimpering. He had already cleansed and dried my damp bottom. I believe he would have nursed me himself had Jehovah made it possible. "What is her name?" he asked with pride.

"Her true name is Oseye, but I know you goin' call her somethin' else."

Although Daddy's beloved mother was named Oseye in honor of her own paternal grandmother, he acted as though there was nothing special in the name. Daddy paused before saying, "How does Sarah sound to you?"

As much as possible, Mama believed in avoiding conflicts. Those with whites could bring beatings, sellings, or worse. Those with her husband wounded the man more than he deserved. Realizing that silence was the greatest assent he could get from her about an American name, Daddy said, "Then Sarah it is."

I lay in silence between them, the child born into slavery whose free-born mother wanted to give her the old country name "the happy one" and whose free-born father thought an American Biblical name might sound better to Jehovah.

It was almost midnight, and Daddy would rise at 4:30 a.m. to eat a little before he walked out to the lower 80 acres which had cost Nathan Prescott's ancestor a legendary sum. Charlotte could sleep an additional fifteen minutes before she joined the weeding crew in the vegetable fields. Daddy held his breath and listened to me nursing. During Mama's pregnancy, she had received only a little more nourishment than her inadequate normal fare. She had a few days off before she rejoined the vegetable crew so I ate until I was content.

"I can hardly wait to see her in full light," said Daddy. "She must be very beautiful."

"She is," said the proud-as-could-be mother.

Daddy left unsaid, "Because you are her mother and everything you touch becomes beautiful." Mama omitted, "Because Nyame made her and she will be adored by this family." All that mattered before first light was that for the time being, we were a complete family.

Sunday morning came and Daddy had the first opportunity to see me in the light, I was six days old. Of course, in his presence, my older brothers and sisters had already spoken about my embarrassingly light skin. Daddy scolded them, "Never forget that our colors come in many shades. Jehovah paints us as He sees fit."

Daddy examined my features, then said to Mama, "Just as I assumed, she is a beautiful angel. We have been blessed."

Knowing that his warrior's heart was breaking, still Mama took her husband's words at face value. Daddy kissed both of my cheeks and walked with me out of the shack, letting everyone in the quarter know, "This is my daughter in whom I am well pleased."

ONE OF THE FEW

Following the Sunday afternoon meal on Fruits of the Spirit Plantation, most of the slaves either worked our allotted small plots to supplement our inadequate diets or rested. Daddy was the exception. He devoted most of his time to making shoes. My brother Robin worked beside him, even before he was old enough to go to the fields. I doubt that Robin was initially given a choice, but he preceded the rest of us in despising our condition. The master's ongoing abuse of Mama helped our older brother realize that the more efficient he became, the sooner all of us would be able to escape. Robin was a great student of his craft.

Near the cobbler workplace, one cool autumn Sunday, I read a book with my back against a gorgeous tree. Daddy and Robin neared completion of a pair of shoes in preparation for Judge Grimes' arrival. Robin's favorite girl came timidly to the workplace and said, "Mr. Kofi, sir."

Daddy looked up from his work and said, "Kenneth." Immediately he went back to work.

"I keep forgetting, Mr. Kenneth, sir."

"Speak up, child, we are hard at work."

"Could I have a word with Robin?"

"He has ears."

Eve was silent, thinking of how to make clear it was privacy she desired. After several seconds she said, "Just a word." She glanced at me fearing I already knew something that would take me years to learn.

Daddy deeply sighed. Never looking up, he said, "'A' indicates one but I suppose you mean a few."

"Well yes, sir."

"Go," he said to Robin who had not dared to even honor Eve's presence.

"Back soon, Daddy." Robin hopped up.

This time, our father looked up. To Robin he said, "The sentence should be, 'I shall return post haste, Father'."

"Excuse me, sir," said Robin, before repeating Daddy's words.

He and Eve stepped out of Daddy's hearing range. Still she whispered something in Robin's ear. I could see him swallow hard and flush red. He said something and she nodded forcefully. Robin returned, clearly shaken.

"Should you be telling me something, son?"

"No, sir, I don't guess."

"You don't guess?"

"No sir."

Daddy had completed Robin's work, put an initial shine on both shoes and begun cutting the leather for a new pair. He stopped his work. "Listen to me good, son. This is not a new message, but you and your brother Dan are what is called women chasers. I understand the attraction, but do not fall in love. I repeat, do not fall in love. I am struggling to save enough money to free our family. A new addition…or maybe two, would mean additional time spent in bondage for, to marry one of my children would make that person and any offspring a part of our family. Do you understand me, son?"

Robin was the hardest man I had ever known, but that day he swallowed and softly said, "Yes sir."

"Now give the finishing shine to these shoes."

Daddy and Robin had worked several hours before Judge's visit. Daddy called for a short break and came in to kiss Mama, who was knitting simultaneously with four needles, two made with bone wire and two from straight tree branches. Daddy played with his younger children. Because each night Daddy alternated working on shoes with periods of teaching either Latin or English, he never felt that play stole from the coming emancipation time from the family. "Besides," said Daddy, "my children have to know me as more than the man who orders or teaches them."

If I had been Robin who was denied play time, I would have found a way to talk my way into the foot races, jump rope games, and the like. Nobody ever heard Robin complain to Daddy. If and when Daddy said "Do" Robin did. Daddy had some practices that Robin rejected, but in powerful ways my brother valued his love and approval. Daddy was playing a Latin word game with Dan and me— needless to say I was winning—when everyone looked up to the sound of whistling. Enjoying a free man's option, Judge Grimes had arrived later than the appointed time.

Daddy shortened the game and left with Robin trailing. Judge Grimes, Daddy's sales representative, had arrived for his quarterly pickup. A free man of color, he chose to remain in Virginia. With the threat of lynching hovering over the heads of even the most innocent, Judge was profiled a suspect criminal, and in 1806, together with every other free Virginia person of color, he had been forced to put up a bond should he break the law. Judge dressed with the realization that his social status was precariously balanced. Consistently his clothing was too fine to be that of a slave's, but not so fine as to draw a caning by a poor white. Regardless of the weather, he wore a scarf around his neck, hoping to hide the place where he had been branded just above his right collar bone. Daddy once told Robin that it was his knowledge of Judge's background that gave him enough respect to trust him with the shoes that held our family's future.

Judge had purchased his own freedom in 1800, discarding *Dama*, his Mandingo name. Whites had always either pretended *Dama* was unpronounceable or called him Damn or Dame. He had thought that he outmaneuvered those who disrespected him by having his official name recorded as Judge Grimes. To his consternation, instead of using the name that should have brought deference, few whites or colored people addressed him as "Judge." Whites consistently called him "boy" or "nigger." Blacks addressed him as Grimes, the name he had taken from his last slave master who had treated him exponentially better than had the previous ones.

The children younger than Robin came out to look at one of the greatest wonders in our narrow world: a free walking black man. "You's a good daddy, Kenneth," said Grimes. "These children look at you like you was the Apostle Paul."

"Do not be sacrilegious, Grimes."

Grimes laughed good naturedly. "Don't know the word, but as a free man, since the white man ain't said, don't be that, I guess I can be whatever it's supposed to mean."

Daddy let the matter drop. "I've four pairs of boots and twelve pairs of shoes."

Grimes bent over and suddenly kissed my forehead. Then he saw Mama. "You looking fine as ever, Miss Esi: dark as a lark, pretty as a kitty."

"Thanks for the compliment, Judge. You looking spry yo'self," she said before returning to the shack. All except Daddy, Robin and me took her movement as a signal to follow suit. Since she had not spoken an order, I stretched the issue. Judge fascinated me.

Daddy guided the conversation back to business. "About the boots and shoes—"

"Slave shoes?" Grimes interrupted.

"All my shoes are first quality. You may sell them to whomever you wish, but you know that before the harvest I do make servant shoes for others on our grounds. Those can never be sold. They are for use here."

"If I was a gambler, I'd bet my plantation—"

Daddy took his turn at interrupting, "You do not own a plantation."

Judge laughed and said, "You're right, I don't. What I own is a store. I'd bet my store against a peach that cheap ass Prescott pays you a whole lot less for them slave shoes than I do."

While keeping his eyes on his work, Robin hung on every word Judge uttered, but Daddy saw Judge as a free man who was too content with the status quo. He believed that if Judge had embraced the language and gone north to Philadelphia, a place he had once heard was The Holy Experiment, the merchant could have become great. Normally Daddy steered clear of any interactions with Judge that went beyond giving him the product. If he ever told Judge what he saw in him, Robin did not report it. Judge told Daddy how much he deemed each pair of boots or shoes was worth, but he had to give Daddy's money to Prescott who credited Daddy an unspecified percentage on the ledger. Sporadically Prescott would report to Daddy how much was in his savings. Accounting questions were forbidden. Everyone knew the rules of the game, and as long as things remained ordered, life flowed without waves.

That day Daddy must have been thinking about freedom even more than usual. To feed an inner need, for the first time he set aside the surname and addressed his representative as the man desired. "Judge, what do you like most about freedom?"

I stopped pretending to be reading and listened intently. Judge, who could neither vote nor testify in court, and had to carry his manumission papers to the outhouse, lived for this question. "The goodest part of freedom," he said, "is not havin' somebody tell me to go to bed, get up, or if I can walk down the road and court the woman I chooses to court."

Even at 14, I knew the last right was hyperbolic. If the woman were a slave, a free man of color still needed her master's permission to make a social call. Both men understood this caveat, and it went unchallenged. All Judge had needed to exhibit was a single choice beyond to live or to die, and he would have shamed Daddy's options.

"The air, life…do they taste different?"

"I ain't sure I knows what you mean."

"Walking about, does the feel in your mouth make an ear of corn or a pork chop taste different than it did on a plantation?"

Emphatically Judge said, "Brother, free ain't all it's cracked up to be, but I'd rather be free than not. To tell the truth, the years I was slavin' for Mister Charlie, the only thing that kept me goin' was my woman and my kids. If'n I hadn't been workin' for Minnie and the boys, I would've killed myself."

Daddy could have said, 'You must be reading my mind; my family is all that keeps me going.' Instead he said aloud, "I want to give you something extra." He went into our house and returned with a pair of boots that he had kept aside to wear on the day of his own freedom. He polished them frequently, so even if he had cared, Judge could not have known they had been made years before.

"Man, you ain't gotta do that for me," protested Judge. "You pay me well."

They both knew Daddy was blind to how much Judge was being paid. "I know I don't have to give you the boots, but everything I can make you sell. This is a small bonus for seven years of faithful service."

Judge overlooked the implication that he, a free man, was a

27

servant to a slave. He simply extended his hands for boots worthy of being taken to Monticello. As he was saying, "Thank you, Jesus," Daddy extended his right hand to shake Judge's. Robin believed it was the first time during their relationship that they had touched. Even their original agreement had not required a handshake: Prescott was the guarantor, and the master shook hands only with white men. Legally it was pointless for the two men to shake. By law, a contract was a signed agreement between two white men. Simple rules for a simple people.

"You mentioned Jesus," said Daddy. "Are you a Christian?"

"One of the few," said Judge.

During their conversation, my brother Robin continued working, seemingly oblivious, but favoring both the tone and language of the free man. Aside from his longing to be free, Robin found nothing attractive about Daddy's assimilationist leanings. I wondered what Robin thought of Judge's acceptance of Christianity. Perhaps Judge had tempered his statement enough to simply prove Robin's point: in our world of perpetual drama, practitioners of truth were rare.

FREEDOM SEEKERS

The country celebrates 1776 as freedom's marker. The year was almost twenty years before my parents were kidnapped in Fante-land and brought to America. In Africa their ancestors had known nothing other than freedom. But when the War for Independence ended with an American victory, for slaves it meant only insult sealed with being listed as 3/5 a person. No vote. No freedom. "No rights which the white man is bound to respect." Instead of being welcomed as immigrants invited to enjoy liberty and justice, Esi and Kofi arrived as 12 year-olds in chains. Worse yet, Mama was subjected to rapes that no court in the land would prosecute.

For me, 1827 is my 1776. It was that year when the rapist and slave master, Nathan Prescott, died. His will stated that together with my older brothers Robin and Dan, we would be sent "temporarily" to his Quaker cousin's home north of his plantation in Culpeper, Virginia. This would be my third trip to the Hoge farm. To protect Prescott's investment, four of us had been sent to the Hoges during the 1819 influenza attack that had killed two of our siblings. Five years later, I had been "loaned out" to them for two years. Without informing Prescott, the Quaker couple had allowed me to attend the fully integrated Goose Creek Friends School.

I had never known how long I would be with them. Ever the optimist, when we arrived in 1827, I prayed we would do more than help with the harvest. Although I knew Robin hated all things American, I imagined we three would be able to receive formal schooling to supplement what our father had taught us. Daddy had learned both Latin and better English than is known by most American presidents because the bored master had wanted him as a study partner on a plantation where the only other white man was the overseer. I even dreamed that vacations would be spent with our family back on Fruits of the Spirit Plantation. Silly me.

Already on the road to the Hoge farm were the African-Shawnee, Caesar, his Monacan wife, Monni and the young Quaker boy, Charles Ferguson. Clark and Mary Crispin Ferguson had gladly let their 14 year-old son go on the supervised trip through the woodlands because they knew that Caesar and Monni looked at Charles as a surrogate son.

Caesar and Monni spent most of their time teaching Charles woodland skills and the true history of the land. Occasionally they visited Indian villages and even a few American settlements. Charles had grown up in a Quaker community where he had learned little of the poor treatment of Indians. Beyond the fact that as long as he could remember, his family had harbored freedom seekers fleeing bondage, which demonstrated their conviction that it was evil. He had no direct experience with slavery. They journeyed as far as Georgia. On the return to Charles' parents, Caesar led the trio to Tyler and Mary Pool Hoge's home in Northern Virginia. Mary Pool greeted them. "I have two letters, one sent by thy mother, Charles, and the other from Patience Starbuck. The renowned correspondent recommends, 'please, feed him well; he is a boy with an appetite'."

"It means," said Caesar, "if it can be chewed, he'll bite it." Everyone laughed, and he offered the Hoges a few pounds of maple sugar wrapped tightly in a deerskin cloth.

"Thee hast brought quite a treat," said Mary Pool. "What apple pies I shall make of this."

"She never cooks with slave made sugar," said her husband. "Honey is good, but thy maple sugar is sure to be even better with the apples."

At supper the two of us served the visitors what Charles considered good Quaker fare: beef stew, summer squash, minutes-old corn on the cob boiled in milk, warm bread, freshly churned butter and peach preserves prepared and canned by my own hands during my last stay with the Hoges.

I sat at the side of the table, next to Mary Pool. Charles, with his long plait flowing down from his beaver hat and riding his buckskin shirt, looked more like a bumpkin than a seasoned woodsman. I thought him pretentious and quite amusing but was too well mannered to actually laugh in his face. He continually found reasons to steal glances my way and asked repeatedly for the corn that was stationed at my end of the table. However, while the adults carried on the conversation, he said nothing, forcing me to only wonder about his lack of intelligence without finding a reliable way to gauge it.

"Patience Starbuck writes that she moved from Philadelphia to Waynesville, Ohio," said Mary Pool. "Caesar, did thee and Monni know her before she arrived in Ohio?"

"Never heard tell of her, ma'am, but we know her now," said Caesar.

"She's a good woman," said Monni. "She joined the runaway assistance folk as soon as her house was built."

"I'm not surprised," said Mary Pool. "Friends in Philadelphia say she is one of the most active Friends in helping runaways. They believe her wealth is limitless."

"I don't know nothing about that kind of money," said Caesar. "I try to measure folk on what they deliver to help the struggling. I can say that I like how she makes a room feel, and how she ain't scared to help neither brown nor red."

Mary Pool and I cleared the dishes, and Caesar left the table to go outside to smoke his pipe. Charles excused himself and joined his mentor. "Did thee see that mulatto girl?" said Charles.

"There are no mulattoes; only people," said Caesar.

Somehow Charles had forgotten that Caesar IV was descended from several Native American peoples and also had both African and European bloodlines. As well, he was married to a Monacan who had a trace of the same Irish ancestry found in the Ferguson family. There was nothing intelligent Charles might add, so he waited patiently for Caesar to finish his pipe. The two returned to the dining room and found me drying the dishes that Mary Pool and Monni had washed.

"Girl, what is thy name?" said Charles.

Convinced that his dull scissors would never touch my cloth, I looked at him while I slowly dried the penultimate dish. Then I turned my back to pick up the last dish. Mary Pool had taught me, "There is that of God in everyone and thee is equal to anyone." How dare this strange, rude boy approach me directly!

Charles retreated a few steps away. He could not take his eyes off me. I dried the final dish, looked him in the eyes and deliberately walked right past him. He recognized a fragrance which he would one day learn was jasmine. I wore it regularly, for my own pleasure not for some strange boy's who had a funny northern accent that made him sound stupid.

Mary Pool, who had forgotten to formally introduce us, pretended not to notice my snub. She said graciously, "Forgive me, Charles, this is Sarah."

Meanwhile, Caesar and Tyler both laughed. "She did not like thy tone, Friend Charles," said Tyler. "I beseech thee to be more considerate."

Embarrassed, Charles excused himself from the room.

"Would thee enjoy a tumbler of my rye or a little peach brandy?" Tyler asked Caesar.

"I might enjoy it," said Caesar, "but it don't agree with my thinking. My daddy used to say 'a clear head is worth more than a good gun'."

◊◊◊◊◊◊

My brothers honored my request and waited for me at the well in the back yard. When I arrived, they were just finishing one of their absurd conversations concerning the efficacy of Fante polygamy, the only piece of old country culture that interested Dan. "Two women is plenty for me," said Robin. "The ones I named is the best in the county."

Dan replied, "If I could have as many wives as I wanted, I can't imagine having less than three. I'll take Carolina, Zephyrine, Tillie Mae, Roberta..."

"You boys can be so sickening," I interrupted them and filed away the fact that most names on Dan's list varied, but Zephyrine's always came up whether he filled his fantasized harem with as many as six or as few as three.

"Speaking of sickening," said Dan. "I almost had to speak to that new boy, Charles."

"Why?" said Robin balling up his fists. "He put his hands on Sarah?"

"No!" I exclaimed. "Leave me alone, both of you. He may be rude, but his manners are better than yours."

"Just because we plan on having more than one woman?" said Dan laughing.

"You better hope you can find somebody who'll suffer a smart mouth gal like you," said Robin, joining in the laughter.

"I didn't come out here to be teased," I said. "I just want to make sure I can sleep in that room without anybody *including you two* teasing me." Dan started to make a joke, but I quickly said, "I don't want to have to tell Mama on either one of you." I already had more than enough evidence to ensure their conviction, and every time I gathered a new piece, I made certain they knew it was in my possession.

"Like I told Zephyrine, don't worry, I'll be good," said Dan before bursting into laughter that this time Robin did not join.

"Sometimes you two are like giggly little girls," I said quieting the air.

"That wasn't me this time," said Robin.

◊◊◊◊◊◊

The most recent visitors were offered space in the barn loft. Monni spoke for them all. "We've been sleeping with the rest of nature for three weeks. Don't worry about us."

The Hoges deferred, but Mary Pool said before the guests retired, "Monni, after I share something with thee, please, would thee tell the children a bedtime story?"

We six 'children' were as old as Robin's 19, but Monni spoke briefly with Mary Pool and accepted the assignment.

Their four sons, my brothers and I filled the Hoge beds. The boys were home on harvest vacation from Fair Hills Friends Boarding School. They were crammed two to a bed while, wearing a quilted robe borrowed from Mary Pool against prying eyes, I enjoyed one to myself. Because the window did not open, and the night was warm, there was little ventilation. In the August heat of Virginia, I perspired as much as if I were in the fields.

"Long ago and very near where we are tonight, Hawk the grandmother, sat on a turtle…"

Monni finished her story, and left us.

Daddy tried hard to make us Americans for the imagined jubilee. He had regularly taught those of his children who chose to learn. Dan and I studied Latin and English on Sunday afternoons and several evenings during the week. Robin sided with Mama who desired to go back to Africa and rejected the notion that blacks would ever be accepted in this hateful country. She deliberately butchered the overlords' language. When Daddy was not around, Robin did the same.

Before candles were extinguished, Robin left the room to go to the outhouse. "Like the pig said to the horse, 'I gotta do what I gotta do'. Be back directly, li'l brother," he said to Dan.

One of the Hoges said to Dan, "Why does he talk funny?"

"What do you mean?" said Dan.

"He doesn't sound like you—"

Another Hoge interrupted, "Maybe he's the one that talks strange, especially for a slave."

"Are you two half-brothers?" said the initial questioner.

"Half does not exist," said Dan. "We are raised in the same house by the same parents. We are as whole as—"

"Jacob and Esau," said the boy who had interrupted his younger brother.

Dan stared him down. "As you and your brothers."

The oldest of the Hoge brothers came to his siblings' defense. "They were not trying to offend. The differences are so pronounced that even these two could not overlook it."

Dan was darker than midnight and Robin lighter than the palm of my hand. Was he speaking of skin color as well as language?

"Find a way to overlook it," said Dan, "as I find a way to overlook your blond hair and your brother's brown hair, the one over there's gray eyes and the other's blue eyes."

Robin returned, hearing from the ladder, only the end of Dan's menacing advice. After he had nearly jumped up the last two steps, he said, "Y'all been talkin' 'bout me?" Two Hoge boys blew out their candles simultaneously, no one speaking a word. "Y'all be disrespectin' me, and I'll be all over you Quaker boys like oats on a mill floor."

I could hear their heavy breathing and feel heat rising. I waited in the silence, prepared to intervene. Multiple snores allowed me to relax. My mind turned to the social advantages the boys had over me. Just when resentment reared its head, it occurred to me to take Vergil's advice, '*collige virgo rosas*,' I said to myself. Gathering roses made supreme sense. I would not be shut out from joy. I wondered what that reprobate, Nathan Prescott, might say if he could read my mind from wherever the evil go when they die. Surely he would see a girl who did not dream of spending her life in slavery or serving louts in heaven. Catching myself, I wondered why the evil occupy so much of our thoughts. Robin loved saying, "Forget you. Forgot you. Never thought about you." That lie did not serve me well so, as Daddy would have, I prayed that Jehovah would forgive me my weakness.

◊◊◊◊◊◊

As they prepared for bed, Monni said to Caesar, "*Psai-wi ne-noth-tu.*"

Hearing himself called true warrior, Caesar replied, "*Lenawe nilla.*"

By declaring himself Shawnee, Monni knew he was willing to strip and lay down with his eyes closed. Once in place, without needing a light, she kissed one-by-one each of the ten battle scars on his body. The wounds coursed from his forehead all the way down to a calf cut by a Choctaw tomahawk hurled at too great a distance to cause serious harm. Caesar said in Monacan, his wife's first tongue, "You bring me joy."

Charles had not slept in his parents' room since infancy. He was fascinated by their willingness to be intimate even though he was only a few feet away. Because they preferred native tongues over that of the invaders' they had already taught him enough of their first tongues that he could understand the conversation. Before leaving Ohio, his mother had instructed him to honor their privacy. He turned his back and fantasized.

Caesar was always aware of the battle scars. Over the years, they had become a double positive. His wife cared for them tenderly, believing she encouraged him to forget them. Secretly, he treasured each as a lesson learned. Also, they often forecast bad weather.

The couple's actions moved too slowly for a boy who had traveled more than forty miles that day only to be mistreated by a colored girl that evening. He fell asleep.

In the middle of the night, one of Caesar's wounds started throbbing and soon was joined by a few others. Charles' return from relieving himself long after midnight fully awoke the warrior. Caesar said to his wife, "Monni, do you smell the rain?"

"It's coming," she said drowsily and rolled her back toward him, silently giving him the option of returning to sleep or holding her spoon-style. They fell back to sleep in an embrace.

Later Monni opened her eyes and found her husband lying on his back quietly beside her. Years later, when he told me of this evening, Charles claims he too was awake, thinking of me. He heard Monni say in Shawnee, "Are you awake?"

"Yes," said Caesar before rolling over to face and kiss her in what might have been expectation of a closer bond.

"Mary Pool gave me a package not to be opened until the next time we're in Ohio and said something you need to hear." Caesar stopped kissing and sat up for the news. "Those colored children's parents are being sold tomorrow."

"Do they know?"

"No."

"Are they living nearby? Can we save 'em?"

"They're from Culpeper; you know how dangerous that area is. There are too many whites, bad ground, and few safe houses. A rescue attempt would be too risky, but maybe without implicating the Hoges, we can help the ones here escape."

Charles did not realize what she meant by bad ground, but if this were his chance to be a warrior, Quaker peace testimony or not, he thought he was ready.

For several moments, they were lost in thought. Returning to the topic introduced earlier, Monni said in English to make sure the boy heard her, "Soon there'll be a big storm coming from the south with great wind and rain."

Caesar was a man who always sought opportunity. "It'll be a great cover," he said. "Can you get the three of 'em out without waking the Hoges?"

"Yes." She was away.

"Charles, start wrapping up these blankets, and I'll get the horses."

Although Monni moved as silently as a feather, I suspect Mary Pool had deliberately planted the thought of her and Caesar facilitating an escape, and that the Hoges only pretended to sleep. Why else would she have shown Monni where she stored the pair of her son's castoff pants that she had had me try on, "since thee is about the same size as that youngster to whom I plan to give them"? As for the package, I would discover that it was the journal that I had kept the second time I had stayed with her. When I had learned that I was being pulled out of Goose Creek Friends School and returned to Fruits of the Spirit slave plantation I had been so shaken that I had forgotten it at her house.

Monni gathered us. Caesar said a prayer of thanks and for safety. We were off. We three freedom seekers made a pact. "So long as we black," said Robin, "we ain't goin' forget each other."

Dan added, "That means forever."

"That means forever," I repeated. "Three for three. You for me. He for he. She be a tree. Planted by the waters."

"You my main gal, Sister Sarah," said Robin, seizing his unjust right as the oldest to have the last word.

◊◊◊◊◊◊

With me wearing the "borrowed" pants of one of the Hoge boys, we rode two to a horse, Dan behind Caesar, me behind Monni, and Robin behind Charles, despite Charles' offer than I share his mount. Had I answered affirmatively, Robin might have pounded him even before we were on the road. We came to Winchester, Virginia, which once was the site of a Shawnee village. Caesar had us dismount and tie the horses. We took them into a vine-covered cave next to a creek, only a few miles from Judge Grimes's house. Caesar paid his respect to a nearby burial place and led us on foot to the free black man's house.

Judge traveled about half the time, leaving his wife and a hired man to run their general store which specialized in goods made by slaves like my father who were trying to purchase their freedom. Protocol dictated that even in this store, whites were served first. Caesar explained that Judge made so little profit on his wares that people traveled for miles past other stores. A few of the whites who did so helped runaways. If he had white customers, we could not stop. Who could tell at a glance which whites were trustworthy and which were kidnappers or informants looking to turn a profit on our misfortune?

Caesar waited until after official closing time at the store. He spied a candle shining in the northwest window, indicating that Judge was at home and the way was clear. The rest of us remained with Monni while he gave Judge notice by knocking on the back door. Judge answered, and we were waved up. Thoroughly soaked, we dripped pools onto the dirt floor as we rested in Judge's cellar near the entrance to a tunnel that ran to the cave.

"Who these chillen be?" Judge asked.

"They're from Fruits of the Spirit down near Culpeper," said Monni.

"I know the place. Kenneth should be called Kofibe y'all's daddy?"

"Yes, sir," we answered together.

"I been knowin' yo' daddy a long time. Uppity, stupid to trust Prescott, but fair," said Judge with conviction. "I thought I recognized y'all, especially this pretty one. You must be the one who used to have them fat cheeks and like readin' them books. You a 'Daddy's gal', aint't you?"

I sorely missed my father and smiled at the compliment.

"That rain done wet y'all so much I couldn't hardly tell child from hoppity frog," Judge laughed. We quietly waited for his next words.

"A few years back, Kenneth gave me a finer pair of boots than any he ever sold the masters. I don't wear 'em nowhere but to meetin'. Heard y'all's master up and died."

"Yes, sir," said Robin.

"Cracker owe me money," said Judge. "Bet I don't see a penny of it; probably had it buried with his cheap ass. Take, take, keep. That's all they know. Take, take, keep. How come y'all runnin' by yourself?"

Robin answered from what he had been told by Monni. "The rest, they bein' sold right now."

"I hope they go as one," sighed Judge.

"With us here, that can't happen, sir," said Dan.

"Heaven help us all," said Judge. "We can't stand here jawin'. Tell me all y'all need," he said to Caesar.

"We don't have time for sleep," said Caesar. "We just need some provisions, and a place to change outta these wet clothes."

"You come to the right place," said Judge, "but I see these chillen ain't wearin' sherryvallies, I'll throw in some. Missy, you ain't too much a woman to wear sherryvallies, is you?"

At thirteen and on the run, despite my budding figure, I answered, "It's muddy out there, sir. I won't mind protecting these trousers."

"You can talk that talk, can't you gal?" he said before calling his wife Minnie to the landing. Because of an 1806 law, she was legally Judge's slave. If he had manumitted her, she would have been required to leave Virginia as their children had done. The same law closed the door to our father using the money he earned from making shoes almost every waking hour that he was not in the fields. He could not free us piecemeal if he had desired to.

"I guess you children are on your way north?" said Minnie.

"Yes, ma'am," I answered.

"How I wish we were going with you," she said softly before hustling away to fill some potato sacks with fruit, salt pork, deer jerk, and biscuits triple-wrapped in brown paper against the rain.

"Minnie don't understand that we's called to make sacrifices, so's we can help folk down here," said Judge. "Life ain't always 'bout your own freedoms. Somebody gotta make a stand in the midst of evil."

I knew Minnie Grimes's status from Daddy. I respected her sacrifice more than her husband suggested he did, but neither of us runaways replied. Judge noticed Charles trying to shrink in the corner. The Quaker had never been around rough talking people of color, and in his home, where he was free to be his cantankerous self, Judge spoke in a way befitting his chosen name. "Come over here by this light, son." Charles obliged, and Judge said, "I'll be! How happen you and Monni runnin' with a white boy, Caesar? He a runaway

Shawnee now, wearin' them buckskins? Outta the light I thought he was just high yellow. Or Prescott done took to slavin' his own?"

"You know that's against the law," said Caesar, ignoring most of Judge's questions. "He's Clark and Mary Crispin Ferguson's son, Charles. Clark was reared around here, but like most of the Quakers, moved up to Ohio."

Judge studied Charles' face. "You look just like them Fergusons. They must've changed to Quakers up north because they wasn't soft down here. Boy, I been knowin' yo' people for years. I even hunted two or three times with the granddaddy you must be named after. I ain't seen no white boy who could shoot like him. Seen him knock a squirrel's eye out just by splinterin' the bark near him on a tree. Damndest trick I ever seen! Let me tell you this before witnesses: just because Jackson ain't worth a ant's leavin', don't get confused and start believin' all Scots-Irish is bad. Don't let nobody mess up yo' mind about yo' people."

"You know everybody, Judge," said Monni.

"Don't believe that lie, honey," said Judge. "I know people that can make me money and the ones that know the Lord. That's all Judge know. Folk like Jackson that might shoot me in the back, I just know *about*."

Before we continued on our journey, Millie gave us a meal of mulled cider, pancakes and bear bacon that Caesar had taught Judge to make years before.

"A word of advice," said Judge. "This rain ain't good for nothin' but runaways. We know it; so do the paddyrollers, and for some strange reason they don't trust the Judge." He laughed before adding, "They think a nigger get free, and he begin thinkin' all niggers need to be free. Any fool know that much when he come out the womb. Come sun, they be out like flies in a pig yard. Don't be nowhere around here then."

"We'll be long gone, Judge Grimes," said Monni.

"'Fare thee well' said Minnie." My grandmama said her Quaker mistress used to say that, "Fare thee well, and say hello to freedom for me."

NORTHERN DREAMS DENIED

His escape from slavery had cost my brother Robin a great love. Robin prided himself on being strong, seldom talking about what hurt him most, including losing Eve. How much that loss watered the bitter seed within him, I'll never know. But with our joint escape, I could no more distance myself from him than I could from my own skin. With most things he lashed out with biting sarcasm. With her loss he used other women as though they had less heart than trees. One woman that he visited lived on Bluestone Road just north of Cincinnati. Once Priscilla's family had lived in the heart of the city. The growing racial animosity, fed by Ohio's Black Codes, especially the ridiculous $500 bond each black was supposed to post against the expectation of a first arrest, led her father to leave laboring in the pig slaughtering industry. He contented his family with farming a small piece of land once cleared by the Shawnees. As he predicted, race-based attacks stepped up in the late 1820s. Whites new to Cincinnati saw those on top living like European royalty and grew angry. Few blacks were financially comfortable, but enterprising or not, we were seen as a risk to the white pursuit of the American dream. Politicians seized the moment and claimed poor whites were being impoverished because blacks were taking jobs that were rightfully theirs. Adding to the insult, we were accused of demanding such low wages that white remuneration was reduced.

Less than two years after I had made my escape north with two of my brothers, the bully boys of Cincinnati began mob violence against blacks.

"Damn, we ain't safe nowhere south of Canada," said Robin to my brother Dan.

Before Dan could answer, I said, "I like it here in Waynesville."

"Unless you go to Quaker meetin' in the middle of a passel of Fergusons, since we came here, you ain't moved two farms on either side of Clark and Mary Crispin's," said Robin.

"And you are not a man," said Dan. "We black men are the ones they hate. You, all they want to do is—"

"Don't go there!" said Robin to Dan. It was a timely warning, because I was one word from slapping him with all the force of the Lord.

No more words were spoken at that time. My brothers went back to the Fergusons' fields, and I to continue learning the seamstress trade as a sort of apprentice to Mary Crispin. Daily I prayed the matter would fade away like weak coloring applied to the dress of an ancestress.

I was wrong. Random beatings, scattered rapes, and a few lynchings preceded half the colored people of Cincinnati, Ohio to be driven out. A large group of the refugees made camps near where Robin's lover lived. Robin came home late one Sunday and told us that Priscilla's father was thinking of joining the caravan heading north to Wilberforce, Canada.

According to Robin, "The old man said, 'Niggers need to go where it's safe'."

The logic made sense, but the implications were too much for me to embrace. "Why should I worry myself trying to please those who hate me no matter what I do?"

"Just let me sleep, gal." Robin wrapped himself in his blanket and turned his back.

I lay awake remembering a conversation between Mary Crispin and her best friend, Patience Starbuck. Patience had said, "Thee did right to give freedom seekers sanctuary."

"What else could a Christian do?" said Mary Crispin. "Jesus himself received sanctuary in Egypt when Herod wanted him killed."

"I pray the family of the Lord was treated better in Egypt than the blacks are in Cincinnati. They are expected to smile while being barred from public schools, relegated to the lowest-paying jobs and charged exorbitant rental rates. They must even do so while stepping into the muddy streets whenever the meanest white person comes toward them on the sidewalks."

"I doubt Babylon or Sodom was worse than that city," said Mary Crispin.

"As well," said Patience, "innocent colored people are abused with impunity. That is why I will do no more than visit the pretentious city that claims to be Queen of the West."

As my brothers had pointed out, I had never visited Cincinnati. But overhearing the words of women who had, I thought those cities cursed in the Bible might actually be superior. Also I was aware from the abolitionist tracts that Patience shared with me that several leaders from among our most militant, and most fearful, were in favor of immigrating to Canada or Mexico, if not to Africa. Led by the pompous Henry Clay, both northern and southern whites encouraged such a removal. I hated the idea of going to our parents' Africa where I feared my light skin would make me more a suspect than was already true in America. As for Canada and Mexico, I thought one was fifty degrees warmer than where we had been enslaved and the other fifty degrees colder than where we now resided. Furthermore, what would an unmarried colored woman do as an emigrant? My protector-brothers were women chasers. I prayed that before too long, each of them would be settled some by a good, strong black woman. However, if my prayers were answered, I doubted that those "sisters" would want me as an appendage.

In the morning I said to Robin, "Mary Crispin and Patience Starbuck have led Quakers in raising nearly $500 to help some Cincinnati colored people moving up to Wilberforce, Ontario,"

"Yeh?" said Robin impatiently.

"In two days," said Dan, "Israel Lewis and James Brown are coming to pick up the money."

"And," I quickly added, "you can go with them to Canada."

"They stole the town and everythin' else in these parts from the Shawnees," said Robin. "We got Shawnee friends, not enemies. We belong in Cincinnati as much as any white man."

"You get no argument from me," said Dan.

"I guess, like my friends say, 'if they can't afford to send us all back to Africa, they's goin' run us all up to Canady and make us pay for each step of the way'. I'd just as soon go back to Virginny."

I reached my hand out to Robin. "Brother, you know I love you, but see the good just this once."

"Is you crazy? You see some good in this mess?"

"The Quakers who don't act Quakerly anger you. The bully boys who hurt us anger you. Virginia's slavers angered you."

"Ain't no news in that tale," said Robin.

"Wilberforce is as close as Culpeper, but they are welcoming us. None of us can return to Virginia without being put back into slavery."

In this rare moment, Robin considered my feelings. He chuckled and clapped his hands. Then he grabbed me and danced while singing my song, "Let Your Mind Dance."

My grief at separating temporarily receded. When we were both out of breath, Robin said, "Did you really think, Eve or not, I was goin' back to see that rollin' Hazel River in old Virginny?"

Despite my previous calm rationale to steer him north, I was almost in a panic over losing my brothers. But not so much that I believed Robin would return into slavery for Eve. I never thought of her as an updated Helen of Troy. What I knew for certain was that our parents and siblings had been sold piecemeal, dispersed to parts unknown, while other colored people headed west. If they were able to join the trappers in the mountains, the likelihood of ever seeing my brothers again would be small. Someday I would marry and convince my husband to at least visit Wilberforce.

Robin had learned the cobbler trade from our father. Since Daddy was self-taught and stumbled upon a few bad habits that sometimes crept into his work, I can say with certainty, my brother's work was superior to Daddy's who himself was the best cobbler in the county. Before my brothers left, Patience purchased Robin's entire store of shoes. She also paid him as much for shoes usually made for runaways and free blacks as she did for the several pairs he had previously made for her: top dollar.

◊◊◊◊◊◊

I watched the Cincinnati refugee wagon train heading north away from hostile territory. Everyone wore their most tattered clothing for fear that their Sunday best would end up in shambles long before the long march was over. Most of the men and older children walked. The elderly, pregnant women, and those with tiny children rode in wagons loaded with the limited possessions they could carry away. Other women ambled beside friends or chased toddlers. Through their tears, they tried to make a community amid the baffling chaos.

As a spectator, I wished I could grieve alone, but all of the Fergusons, Patience Starbuck and hundreds of gawkers had their own plans. I was a stranger in a foreign land. I dared not say, "Don't make a pageant of my people's pain." Ours was an age when people gathered to watch public floggings and lynchings. Why not gaze at a parade of outcasts being driven from their homes?

The time came for my brothers to separate from me. Dan hugged me first and ran off before I could see his eyes. Robin was about to attempt the same ploy, but I held him tight.

"I gotta go, li'l sister," he said.

I said, "Please, please—"

"I ain't no ways pleased with nothin'," he said, "but a man's gotta do what a man's gotta do." He shocked me by removing my arms gently before he walked confidently away. I watched him melt into the moving circle.

My eyes were not dry when I said to Mary Crispin, "What did we colored people do to earn such scorn?"

"Oh, child," she put her arm around me, "this is not about color; it is about rebellious hearts turning away from the Light and hating their neighbors."

Later I learned that the citizens of Cincinnati had stolen the homes and personal property left behind. Soon after the eviction, David Walker, our people's first prominent abolitionist, wrote a fiery appeal that I like to think was partially inspired by our degradation in Cincinnati. Truly an insult to one of the oppressed is an insult to all of us as well as to The Lord. But neither those of us in the west, or Walker in the east, could have predicted that a year later the entire population of colored people would be expelled from Portsmouth, Ohio, 100 miles upriver from Cincinnati.

◊◊◊◊◊◊

While making our escape from slavery years before, we had learned that, on the run, the oppressed are most vulnerable. Shadowing the refugees was Bacon Tate, a notorious white slave hunter from Kentucky. The members of his eight-man posse of mercenaries rarely showed themselves during daylight hours. The lone racial exception among Tate's men was an ex-slave named Naphtali Long. Although he was hired in part because he refused to identify with his own, money was his primary motivator. If someone had offered him the chance to be paid for hunting Chinese, Turks or even United States congressmen, I am sure Naphtali would have welcomed the opportunity.

Considering the refugees had been expelled from the area nearest the Ohio River, Tate had every reason to believe that there were a good number of people without manumission or free papers. As for those legally "free," knowing it would be their word against his and if a trial were held, only whites could testify, he could destroy their proof. Kidnapping and re-selling our people held minimal risk.

For the next week, Tate's man, Naphtali, pretended he was one of the refugees, walking the line, chatting with unsuspecting men, patting children on the head, and flirting with unattached women. More than once he crossed paths with my brothers. Robin usually traveled with a half dozen young men who called themselves "The Fante Gang," or worked two of the same women that Naphtali desired. Showing surprising discipline, Dan spent most of the daylight hours around the men in fine clothes, pretending to seek good conversation. In actuality, his daytime eyes were on a more secure future.

People disappeared. Three were taken one by one as they went into the woods to relieve themselves; another while sleeping on the edge of the group, thinking he was making others safe. Others simply vanished. Did some or all of the latter tire of the road and return to Cincinnati or decide to seek liberty and justice in some other place in America? Finally, one evening, Robin was in an embrace with Priscilla when Naphtali slipped up, knocked him out with a rifle butt and used the barrel to drive the wind out of Priscilla's stomach. Upon regaining consciousness, Robin found himself gagged, chained, and about to be placed in a line being driven toward the wrong side of the Ohio River.

Before his kidnapping, Robin had made no secret of his hatred of Jehovah. He later told me that once shackled, he prayed to Jehovah as well as to the Fante God Nyame. He also prayed that the Fante Gang or Priscilla's father would come to his rescue. His prayers went unanswered.

A common phrase was, "Once you're south of Columbus, you're in Kentucky." Of course, since this was formerly an apt geographical description of the northern boundary of Shawnee-land, and more Ohio residents had been born in Kentucky than in their present state, the description was supportable. Although he had stolen eight people from the refugees, and outriders had picked off a few more colored farm children, Bacon traveled at a leisurely pace. He was confident that whatever hatred came his way was mitigated by the laws of the land and the apathy of those of all colors who gave lip service to despising his actions.

For the first day, Robin alternated between fervent prayers and retreating into himself, assuming blame for lack of vigilance. The second day, he remembered that he and Dan had concluded that Daddy had been blinded by a lust for freedom and the love of Mama. A moment later he thought, 'Shucks, Priscilla ain't nothing like Ma. I don't even like her half as much as Eve. I ruined my life for a couple of strokes of pleasure.'

Meanwhile, the other men often were struck with whips, and Priscilla and a second woman were being abused by everyone in the posse except the turncoat Naphtali, who was denied access. Just past Middletown, through Tate's prodding, the youngest victim helped Robin recognize his responsibility to step beyond self-pity. "Do your Christian duty and help this child, boy," said Tate pointing with his whip.

Naphtali unlocked Robin's chains, led him to the designated place in front of the child and secured him to the man in front. Tate oversaw it all and started back to the front of the line. The child whispered, "Mister Robin, sir, why these bad men treating us like this?" She had been brought to Ohio as a toddler. Like most ex-slaves, her parents had refused to tell her anything concerning her past or their own. They had also kept her away from all whites as though each had a fatal disease. Even while the Cincinnati citizens were going through the streets terrorizing the neighborhood, they had foregone attempting to explain the inexplicable. She had not heard the bully boys' favorite saying, "See a nigger, beat a nigger." In fact, she was under the impression that people come in different shades but they are all the same.

Robin tried to conserve his energy, maintain a low profile, and ignore the girl's questions. She was persistent. "Mr. Robin, sir, why they be treating us so mean?"

Finally, Robin attempted an answer, "They don't want us free, baby. They's scared of certain types of freedom."

He had been the only unbeaten man, but he raised his voice at the end of his answer. Perhaps Tate felt the word 'freedom' in one of our mouths was as sacrilegious as saying the Constitution should be burned in effigy. For whatever reason, Tate used his whip, aimed at Robin's neck and brought him to his knees. Several other rapid-fire blows followed until Tate's arm grew weary. The slave line was forced to wait until striped and bleeding, Robin struggled to his feet spitting blood. As soon as he stood, Tate received a new burst of energy and gave Robin a final stroke across his ankles. My brother was sent tumbling on his face.

The child became hysterical. Robin forced himself to say in a croaking voice, "Please, honey, don't cry. I'll be all right."

◊◊◊◊◊◊

The coffle marched through stifling heat. They watched the slave catchers take long, sloppy guzzles of water from their canteens while their own mouths parched. At last they came to a creek crossing and Tate said, "All right men, water the slaves." The kidnapped got down on their knees and drank hurriedly, fearing that on a whim Tate would end the water break.

They reached Covington, Kentucky, and Tate stopped at his mother's for a better meal than the road afforded. "Mama, I'm home," he called out from her front gate. She came running. Tate let her take him in her arms.

"Safe from the wars," she said between tears, perhaps remembering her husband who, according to Tate's fireside boasts, had "taken at least fifty-three Shawnee scalps" during Tecumseh's defeat at The Battle of the Thames.

"It's not that bad, Mama," said Tate kissing her hand. "No bullets were fired." He turned around and in a different voice called to the posse. "All right, boys, do your duty."

Robin said his first thought was that they would be sold right on the porch of Tate's mother's house. Instead, Tate took Priscilla home to be a "house servant", and Robin and Rachel ended up in a nearby slave pen. They were there for several days as periodically more slaves were added to already tight quarters. None of the more than 100 was willing to nurture a relationship with someone unrelated because of fear that whatever community anyone might make would come asunder with the strike of a gavel.

By the time Robin and Rachel were put on the market, he had figured out the merchant's commitment to selling relatives as a unit.

The Tate batch was called to the front. Robin saw Rachel's terror and said, "Wherever we go, baby, from this day on, I'm your daddy."

ALLIES

Charles Ferguson had watched me, a fugitive slave, pull up my dress almost to the knee and dance to "Let Your Mind Dance, Make It True," a song of my own composition.

Quaker, religious restrictions would have placed me, a non-member, off limits even had I been white. Once Charles determined he would cross the Quaker lines and pursue me, he went about putting together an effective strategy. To break through my defenses, he had an inkling that he would need more than both Venus and Cupid could provide. He would need a great deal of luck. I was saving myself for a man blacker than a cloudy night and with hair that, if sprinkled with molasses might appear rock candy.

He studied men with women. No wife or sweetheart seemed more contented with her man than his own mother. After fourteen pregnancies, what was his father's secret? Could it be copied? During the spring of 1830, at 16, Charles noted his father's interactions with his wife, Mary Crispin. Clark was a man of few words, none were nearly as quotable as the weakest line in William Penn's *Fruit of Solitude*. He doubted that his mother heard Clark's words as magical incantations.

After weeks of study, Charles realized that his father's hands were the key. Clark kept a basin of clean water in the barn. Keeping it fresh was as an assignment on the chore list for Ferguson children. Before entering the house, Clark scrubbed his hands until there was not a speck of dirt, even under his fingernails. Upon entering the house, he passed his wife and lightly touched the hair on the nape of her neck or squeezed her elbow. He might come up behind her as she stirred a pot or washed dishes, and touch her in the small of her back while blowing lightly on her right ear. He might simply stand there without speaking and radiate body heat. In response, Mary Crispin might tremble a little. Sometimes she arched her neck preceding a kiss so short that the inattentive might miss it. Periodically Clark placed the whole of an open palm on one of her cheeks.

'Pa's hands are rough as sawgrass,' thought Charles, 'but Ma acts like they're velvet.'

Mary Crispin was a seamstress. If she were sewing, Clark might take the empty chair next to her. While seating himself, he unfailingly placed his right hand on her left knee. Before launching the study, Charles had assumed the chair was either for a daughter wanting to learn something or a symbol that the Holy Spirit was always at her side. He had never seen the hand. After watching his mother redirect children to the chair on the right, it seemed the chair was owned by his father. Clark might plant a kiss and say, "I am truly thankful for thy love," or "Thee is a friend of God." Charles found it puzzling that Mary Crispin, who was infinitely easier around words, rarely replied. Had this been going on under his nose for years?

Once while no one else was around, Charles pretended to read the Bible. From the corner of his eye he saw his father kiss his mother longer than usual and heard her say, "Thee is a riot upon my reason." Although he totally missed what his mother meant, Charles had the wisdom to record it in his journal.

Among other Quaker husbands, not a single one touched a woman except by accident or while helping her into or out of a wagon. They even avoided shaking a woman's hand or giving their adult sisters a hug. Next Charles watched how his father interacted with his daughters. There, with the exception of an occasional elbow squeeze, and kiss on a young one's cheek, his touch was as distant as the average Quaker man. The full palette was reserved and being used for a never-ending painting featuring one woman.

It was time to take personal stock. He was tall for his age, nearly 6 feet and still growing, freckled, and better coordinated physically than he had been prior to being befriended by his Shawnee friend, Caesar IV whose people called him a name meaning "Stalking Panther," and his wife Monni whose traditional name was from the Monacan nation and translated to "Autumn Sunrise." The three trips he had made with them had enabled him to add perhaps five thousand words combined in Shawnee, Monacan, Creek or Cherokee, to English and a sprinkling of Gaelic words passed down through the Ferguson line. He even could understand, although not speak, the slave dialects he had heard in various sections of Virginia, Kentucky, and Tennessee. He had seen the cities of Cincinnati, Richmond, Charlottesville and Chattanooga as well as more than a score of Native American villages. He had met a diverse group of important people from Elias Hicks and Levi Coffin to Black Hoof and John Perry, John Brown and Nat Turner. On more than one occasion I had witnessed him or his brothers hosting boyish contests such as horseshoes games or shooting matches and heard him boast, "I'm not the best, but I am one of them."

The arrogant young scamp felt that he was ready to begin courting me. He chose to follow one of Caesar's maxims, "Kokumethena knows, 'Slow's the way to catch a gator.'" The next time he saw me he squeezed my elbow and said, "Good afternoon, friend Sarah," and continued walking. For a week he limited his contact with me to an occasional elbow squeeze. He was careful to do it whenever he was so moved without paying attention to who might be nearby. He was as nonchalant as his father in a crowd. It embarrasses me to admit, that at this point, I suspected nothing and if anyone noticed during this period, even now, years later, they have not told me.

The next phase was to completely cease touching me for a week. By the third day I would see him and catch myself expecting a touch that did not come. I wondered about myself, 'Why am I so interested in him, and how did this happen? Have I been primed to aspire to a port that may prove too shallow?' I recognized that he was handsome and, at least at home, well mannered, but I saw nothing deep in him. I also suspected that he had vestiges of the wild underneath his Quaker veneer. What was wildness to me? My brothers were unruly, but they knew I was more than a handful. Did this brash Quaker boy underestimate me?

◊◊◊◊◊◊

I had my own small vegetable garden. Periodically I finished weeding and sat between my vegetables and Mary Crispin's flower garden. There, within reach of seven varieties of flowers, sitting with my legs folded, knees together and feet apart, I closed my eyes. I prayed, meditated or even caught a cat nap. I needed that small piece of peace as abundantly as daily I needed the feel of the dirt between my fingers.

One day Charles snuck up within twenty yards of my quiet place and hid behind a huge buckeye tree. He says that he counted seven varieties of butterflies being drawn to the saltwater covering me, but I did not recall ever seeing more than five kinds when I had my eyes open. He says he watched me for ten minutes and "not once did a butterfly rest" on my body. Why should they? I have never been a flower, not like my mother was. But for all the time that he observed, he claimed they flitted around me as though one might choose to taste "the girl blossom." As I was coming out, I felt a gaze and knew that it was his. I slowly opened my eyes and turned toward where Charles had been standing. As silently as a Shawnee hunter, he had disappeared. I wondered, 'Am I imagining things never dreamed?'

◊◊◊◊◊◊

On the eighth day of touch abstinence, Charles casually applied his father's small-of-the-back touch. Although he has never mentioned noticing, the action struck me like a glancing bolt of lightning. There was no doubt in my mind that I wanted more. I understated. I *needed* more.

Because he had yet to approach me directly, he did not realize that already I had fallen in love with him. He convinced himself that there must be another phase to his father's use of touch. He says he was angry at himself because he had listened to his mother before leaving on his trip with Caesar and Monni. If he had paid attention instead of giving them maximum privacy, his education would have been further along. They were more intimate than the average Quaker during the daylight. Surely observing their nocturnal activities would have improved his education.

That night Charles took a greater risk. While all the other children were asleep in the loft, he snuck into the far corner of the master bedroom/dining area. It was on the first floor and surrounded by barrels of flour, molasses, and other commodities. To his surprise, his eyes did not need as much adjustment as predicted. Before lying down, from a special trunk, Clark removed three candles that were bigger than the ones kept in the window. An hour later, his parents fell asleep, and the much wiser Charles climbed upstairs undetected by his siblings. In the morning, I fed the chickens and prayed that the young scamp would walk by. We both had a good idea where we were headed. Charles crossed the yard on his way to the barn.

Looking straight ahead, paraphrasing a line he had heard my brother
Dan use to a local colored girl, Charles said loud enough for me to
hear, "Whatever it is thee seeks, may I help with the search?" That
afternoon, assured no other person was within earshot, he added,
"Thee is a riot upon my reason." The courting began in earnest.

◊◊◊◊◊◊

I became lost in his eyes. Over the years they have changed, but at 16
they were not blue. They were turquoise. *Their* color did not ensure
Charles was a gem. Eyes are only eyes. His spirit interested me. Could
he share it on demand or would he hoard it on whim?

We had a fair idea of where we were. Certainly, I knew that I was
west of my mother's Eden. Place is not enough. What if he thought
we would come together like two streams at the confluence? I had no
intention of being any man's tributary. I needed my own space. We
were aware that the world claimed we were each other's forbidden
fruit, but neither of us heard the voice of God declare, "If you do,
you die." I wanted our lives intertwined like ribs growing out of the
world's cage.

Years ago, I tried to explain this to a well educated sister-in-law
who said, "Sarah, you are mixing metaphors," and I answered,
"Angelica, what else would thee call my life?"

◊◊◊◊◊◊

Several months into the courtship, Charles put his pants on inside
out and was about to leave the boys' bedroom. His brothers burst out
laughing and he asked, "What, may I ask, is so amusing?"

A brother said, "Look at thy pants, Charles." The others laughed
again.

Charles angrily took off his inside-out pants and started over.
"Leave us for a moment," said the senior brother. The others filed

out. "I've seen thee sneaking around with Sarah, Charles. What doth thee think thee is doing?"

"Applying myself to my own business and not thine."

"Has thee forgotten that she is neither a Friend nor white?"

"Has thee forgotten," said Charles angrily, "that thy name is neither Clark nor Mary Crispin and I don't have to ask thy permission for anything?"

"Charles, I'm trying to keep this from the others, but think for a minute. Thee is involved in a denial of customs. Thee is a Ferguson with the birthrights of Crispins, Chubbs, Biddles, and Stocktons, even Penns. Sarah claims her surname is 'Freedom'. Such made up blood has no such birthright."

"Thee and thy concern over birthrights may go the way of wigs on the frontier," said Charles, walking away from his brother. This breach has yet to heal.

◊◊◊◊◊◊

Even after I knew I had fallen in love with Charles, I refused to let his hands do all he desired. I wanted understanding more than loving, respect more than love, a friend more than a lover. Charles had the temerity to point out what he gauged was the depth and breadth of my demands, but lacked the boldness to speak his conclusions. I smiled and said, "I am insatiable."

Was I leading him? Why did he not resist once the goose walked ahead of the gander? Almost from the moment I recognized that I was his answer, I returned him to the place of asking questions. I grew up on a plantation. I knew that his body drove him, but if a man finds himself at a reciprocated point of no return, patience becomes more than a virtue, it becomes a safeguard.

Perhaps I was not as smart as I thought. Charles learned the art of manipulation, even as I refined what I knew of the art of dance. The

Spirit led us to synchronization. We both came under the illusion that for the first times in our lives we alone held our fate.

"I know thee is timid," said Charles one night. I had never considered myself 'timid'. My head rested in the crook of his arm, and this did not seem the time to debate. "Let me protect thee from the world." Before I could protest he added, "My love is like the night, even the summer sun cannot extinguish it." I was impressed with the allusion.

The same brother who first detected our budding romance, claimed that my smile grew in radiance. Before I fully understood the implications, my protector became much more. In July, I recognized that I was pregnant. I was a lone black servant girl. I envisioned myself turned out onto the road, wandering like young black women I had seen before. Maybe someone would offer me a safe haven. Maybe I would be victimized time and time again. I avoided eye-contact, spoke little and was grateful that my morning sickness was light. Finally, I prayed to my mother and learned an ancient courage. However, instead of telling first my 17-year old lover, I went to his 46-year old mother.

'I am at her mercy,' I thought. 'I must come to her corrupt, unable to circumvent the truth that my labors have not all been upright.'

"Mary Crispin, I am—"

"Going to become my daughter-in-law," she interrupted, opening her arms for me to come in. I released the stored-up tension in surprising sobs. Just as I was sure I had fallen, Mary Crispin lifted me higher. "We will see that thee and thy Charles are joined."

Charles's older brother was not the only one who had seen through us. Mary Crispin had noted our actions and considered stopping the love affair. She told me later that by the time she was ready to speak about suspicions she questioned her own motives. She said she went to her friend Patience Starbuck and said, "Am I, of all people, to be tripped by race?"

"But they are mere children," Patience had said.

"Innocents may be permanently hurt," was her reply. "And if I am not Mary Crispin, what shadow have I become? Vision matters."

Another would have claimed I had seduced her son and used the night to send me north like the runaway I was, but Mary Crispin chose the straight path. Refusing to condemn that which she saw as natural, she stood by me and her most headstrong son. She asked me, "In which color would thee like to be married?"

I had spent most of my life as a slave and had not anticipated the question. We sat quietly at the table while Mary Crispin worked on yet another Quaker gray dress. Life went on around us, small children laughing and playing, older ones passing through the room for a piece of bread, or an apple, her daughter, Elizabeth, finding little ways to demonstrate her love for me had not waned.

I turned toward the window. A few diseased leaves had separated from strong mid-summer trees. They floated past the window. "In my youth, Mama lived much of her life in memory. Often, she spoke of the greens of Fante-land and how none were the same. I have forgotten much, but I remember the greens."

Only Elizabeth and I were in the kitchen when Mary Crispin said with a chuckle, "Thee has an eye for Quakers, but unlike most in this sober generation, thee also has an eye for nature's gaiety." She turned somber and added, "Thee knows, Dear Sarah, that the state of Ohio will not recognize a marriage between thee and Charles."

"The 'good state' of Virginia did not recognize the marriage of my parents. We blacks have long accepted that it is for God to bless marriages, not those who by their actions deny Him."

◊◊◊◊◊◊

Mary Crispin asked her husband to take her to Springboro so that she could purchase dress material. On the road she said to him, "As

I've told thee, it seems that thy son Charles is taken with Sarah." Clark waited. "He is taken with her, and she is taken with our grandchild."

A full quarter-century after he had fallen in love with the Quaker maiden who had anchored his seemingly aimless life, Clark knew both about romance and silence. He stopped in the middle of the road and brought his wife into an embrace. From that position, he felt her heart beat against his chest. Years later, he told me it was not pounding hard; thus, Mary Crispin was easy with the changes in the wind. I remain amazed that he never disclosed that weeks before he had caught Charles and me in a compromising position. No one can ask for more than to have both in-laws as allies.

IMPATIENT PATIENCE

Always despised, but usually dismissed as impotent, misguided fools, with Nat Turner's Rebellion, abolitionists were being cast as seditionists because they supported us as equals deserving freedom. The charges came not only from planters. They were joined by many who opposed slavery but hoped for gradual manumission accompanied by black deportation. Hateful attacks silenced many would-be advocates for black inclusion.

The Nantucket-born Patience Starbuck was not inclined to be driven away from any mission. "Sarah, Jesus was executed by the Romans and the good Quaker, Mary Dyer, executed by Massachusetts Puritans," she once told me. "They persevered in the cause of justice. So, shall I."

Patience had been aware of Ohio's racial tensions when in 1826, at age 28, she had arrived in the state. Recognizing that her radical anti-slavery position was at odds even with most liberals, she had chosen Warren County, an area that had been settled by members of the Religious Society of Friends. Her spiritual family members, had forbidden slave owning even before the War for Independence. As an added benefit, Warren County was close to Cincinnati, the Queen City of the West, a place where a bored single woman might be amused.

When I escaped from Virginia, Patience had already been in Ohio for a year. Life on the frontier had made her increasingly thick-skinned. Perhaps that is why she had removed herself from Eastern parlors. No one on the western side of the Appalachian Mountains could steadily resist the mainstream and remain soft.

Her vision was displayed by the makeup of the two men that in 1832 she sent to Cincinnati with orders to fetch guests who had made the long trip from Philadelphia to Ohio. One of her hired men was an Irishman, the other a colored man. The former had spent years as a Hamilton County sheriff's deputy and was thus strategically placed should the need arise to vouchsafe for the free paper of his associate. As was true in my own case, the colored man was a runaway whose passport had been authorized by a judge who openly admired Patience's business acumen. I believe he secretly hoped for some other benefit. If so, he was a slow actor.

I greeted the three Philadelphians at the door. Once inside, Angelina Grimké, a 27-year-old, asked Patience, "Does Ohio always have snow this late in the spring?"

Patience said, "Dear Angelina, the only thing we *always* have is racial hatred."

"I was led to believe that this is a Quaker enclave," said Angelina's sister who shared my first name.

"Sarah Grimké —"

"Why address me as in a letter? Just plain 'Sarah', please," interrupted the guest. "No need for 'Quaker formal' among partners in justice."

Patience smiled broadly. "Grimkés and *Sarah* Douglass." She paused to shake hands with a diminutive colored woman with bright eyes. "I have been reminded of the need to introduce our temporary assistants, Sarah Ferguson and Elizabeth Ferguson. These near neighbors are sisters-in-law."

The law to which she had referred was God's law, the only one she honored. I was in an interracial union making my marriage unsanctioned by man-made, oppressive northern law. Perhaps I would have been more disturbed, but as slaves, man-made, oppressive southern law had denied my parents' marriage. As a culture, the African-American way of viewing the world is to seek validation within and from the Creator.

After acquaintances were made, Patience continued, "To the earlier question about weather, thy coach traveled by way of Cincinnati, a city seated on the slave border and known by many as 'the kidnapping capital of the free world'. I assume the snow of which thee spoke was theirs. Here in our Warren County 'Quaker enclave,' today we have snow-*melt* and sunny skies. Perhaps that portends to better weather universally."

She offered her most cultured laugh and the others joined her. I recalled that Patience had been born into one of New England's wealthiest families and that she had informed Elizabeth and me that the Grimkés were from an upper-class South Carolina family.

The third Sarah, Sarah Douglass, was the first colored woman I had ever met whose education was superior to my own: two years in an integrated Virginia Quaker school and a dozen under my father's tutelage. By her bearing, Sarah Douglass also displayed familiarity with upper class culture. By her dress and speech, she published that she too judged herself a Quaker.

Upon learning of the special meeting, Elizabeth and I had begged for the pleasure of assisting Mandy, Patience's cook. Over the years, Patience had read correspondence to us from several of her abolitionist friends and acquaintances. We had thus heard many opinions from each of the three guests before they arrived. To sit at their feet and learn more about what it meant to be a thinking woman when male mythology claimed we were inferior by nature, we Ferguson women would have volunteered to clean the barn.

"The laborer is worth her pay," said Patience. "If the Bible is clear on anything, it is that laborers should not be cheated." What ex-slave would argue with such a philosophy? Happily, I joined Elizabeth in being paid only slightly less than Mandy.

As pre-arranged, Elizabeth put the guest coats in the room reserved for such and I escorted them upstairs to their assigned rooms. I had enjoyed tea on the first floor several times but not been upstairs in this brick house on the hill since my initial visit following my escape from Culpeper, Virginia. Once we were on the second floor, I was able to admire the tasteful beauty almost as though seeing it for a first time. Patience adored the best of everything, including wood, cloth, glass, and spirit. So long as she purchased from other Quakers, she never felt her furnishings were self-indulgent.

"This is a magnificent house, Sarah," said Angelina.

Signaling that even in Ohio, I would not play the invisible slave's role, I pretended that I thought she was speaking to me. Before her sister, I answered, "It surely is."

The Grimké sisters made eye-contact and laughed lightly. What might have been an awkward moment passed. I could see they were good women. The rooms were well-appointed in quiet elegance funded by the death of Patience's whaling father and brothers. They had been killed by the same sea that had been the foundation of the family's multi-generational financial empire. Patience had greatly improved on their wealth by investing in various businesses while simultaneously giving away more money than my family had dreamed existed. Grimké money had come from the blood, sweat, and dashed dreams of slave labor. To the sisters' credit, they had removed from what they recognized was ill-gained bounty. Now, in full voice and unassailable credibility, they moved among the country's most harsh critics of slavery. Douglass money was the result of two business people. Her father was a hairdresser and her mother a teacher as well as a milliner daughter of yet another colored businessman. I myself was a seamstress with a good enough eye to envy Douglass' exquisite gray silk bonnet with a single scarlet rose extending from a white ribbon.

I left hostess and guests and went back downstairs to assist Mandy and Elizabeth in preparing for the afternoon tea which would follow the Philadelphians' rest. During the interlude, Mary Crispin, my mother-in-law, brought my baby to me for nursing. Together with Elizabeth, we sat enjoying a cup of coffee. Mary Crispin said, "I wonder how the Golden Lamb Inn received Sarah Douglass."

"It is my guess," I said, "that the answer to that question would be: not at all."

She sighed. "I suppose nearly everywhere one turns we find unholy compromise."

Although the Golden Lamb was owned by a Quaker, it catered to whites alone. In 1832, few of their guests would have accepted a colored table-mate. En masse, they also would have removed themselves and demanded a refund had one of us been allowed a hotel bedroom. In keeping with the established national policy, once more our people were sacrificed on money's altar. I desired positive energy, so I entered a silence that my two in-laws also welcomed.

After several minutes of closed eyes meditation and prayer, my mother-in-law took the baby back home with her. Together with Elizabeth, I rose to assist the cook. There was a knock at the door. I found an unknown servant standing with two women.

"May I help you, sir?" I asked.

Without honoring me with a greeting, he stepped aside and two women entered.

"I am Harriet Beecher, and this is Mrs. Barclay who was visiting from London when I was advised by Quakers in the city that I was invited here for the week."

"My name is Sarah Ferguson. Let me show thee inside."

"Thee uses Quaker plain speech?" said the Englishwoman. Instead of waiting for an answer, she continued. "I am pleased to meet thee. I am Margery Lloyd Barclay. I might have come with the Philadelphia party but chose to delay my journey so that young Harriet would not have to travel alone."

Patience came down the stairs, wearing a burgundy dress that made Margery blush. "So thee was neither abandoned by the others nor frightened by traveling through the frontier with cougars, wolves, and bears on the prowl?"

She was teasing. I had lived in this community for five years and could not count five such wild animals in all that time.

Unruffled, Margery Barclay replied, "I am afraid that a single fox and a small herd of deer were the only creatures willing to greet us…and then from afar."

"I am so pleased to see a real-life British Quaker," said Patience still smiling, "and one who knows how to write such substantive letters despite my 'Hicksite leanings'."

"Leanings?" said Margery. "Thee sits deep in the midst of that camp of radical Friends. Fortunately, Friends in England believe that divisions are made to be healed." She turned still more serious. "Will thee need to see my meeting's letter of introduction?"

"Whyever? We've written to each other for years. I feel as though we share an established friendship," said Patience, suddenly turning to Harriet. "And thee must be my friend Lyman Beecher's daughter."

"Yes, I am Reverend Beecher's daughter, Harriet. Father sends his best."

"Splendid. Tea appears to be ready," said Patience. "And in timely fashion, here are my Philadelphia guests."

The Grimkés and Sarah Douglass had descended the staircase and smiled their greetings. While the new satchels were carried upstairs,

Patience said, "I am sorry, that I do not have a castle. There are only six bedrooms to the second floor. The two of you will have to share. I hope that's not an inconvenience."

"Excuse me," said Margery, "but are there not five guests and thee?"

"Yes, five plus one equals six," said Patience. "My cook has her own bedroom. You late arrivals will not mind sharing a bed?"

Margery looked at the Grimké sisters to see if they would offer to accommodate her. The sisters failed to volunteer.

"Then it is settled," said Patience. "Let us wait on the Lord a while before tea."

I was surprised by this exchange because I knew that the room in question had two twin beds. I wondered if this had been a test to see if sharing space were beyond our haughty guest or merely one of Patience's puckish acts.

We all gathered in the parlor, and Patience read the Sermon on the Mount from her family Bible. I knew that she read the Bible regularly but had never seen her do so before entering a period of silence. I assumed that she signaled to the Englishwoman who had no doubt heard the lie that Hicksite Quakers had so elevated the experience of Truth in the present that they had rejected the Bible. We heard what I consider the most beautiful words prior to Shakespeare, then sat in silence for more than twenty minutes. Patience broke the meeting by shaking hands with those seated on her right and left.

"When the Truth occupies our souls, there is a superior eloquence to deep silence," said Sarah Douglass.

"Along with Quaker commitment to justice, the silence is what first attracted me to the Religious Society of Friends," said Sarah Grimké.

"Would that Philadelphia Friends received me and other people of color in such a way that the silence could be better appreciated," said Sarah Douglass softly.

Initially no one directly touched the subject of Quaker segregation. Eventually, Margery made a feeble pass at it by saying, "I am told that the colored people of America prefer singing and preaching."

"We 'prefer' justice," said Sarah Douglass, "especially when it flows from those who profess to embrace it."

Spurred by Sarah Douglass' words, Angelina said, "It grieves me that Philadelphia Quakers most often choose to accompany colored people to back benches and station sentries posing as ushers to monitor their coming and their staying."

"Now that Pandora has escaped the box," said Patience, "our local meeting is not at unity with such behavior. My house was built on the frontier for a purpose."

We servers waited until the room settled and left to carry out our assignments. Upon our return, Patience said, "And what dainties do we have this fine afternoon, Mandy?"

"Black, gunpowder, or ginger tea along with apple fritters, gingerbread, and crullers," said Mandy who rolled a food cart just behind Elizabeth's matching cart with the service and teas which I served.

"Please save room for a small treat afterwards," suggested Mandy.

"And if I may, I will add to such treat," said Margery.

Having pinched a few desserts while still in the kitchen, the svelte Mandy enjoyed only a single cup of tea and left us to continue preparing supper. Seconds later Elizabeth and I rose to set the table before clearing the tea dishes. When we returned to the gathering, it was with trays of rice flour sponge cake accompanied by a small dollop of lemon custard ice cream.

"The rice flour is in honor of those with Southern roots," said Patience, "although it was both grown and milled by free laborers."

"Thank the Lord for free trade goods," said Sarah Grimké. "Too much honoring of roots can sometimes dishonor the fruits."

Patience said, "Had I been among Protestants I would have said, "Amen."

"Thy servants are well schooled," said Margery. "The finger food was delectable and the ice cream—"

"Be forewarned," said Patience. "Mandy may well be the best cook west of the Appalachians, but it was I who made this honey sweetened, lemon custard ice cream." The guests laughed and she added, "Otherwise there might have been more than a mere tablespoon each!" They continued making merry while Elizabeth and I again cleared the service.

"And here," said Margery, "all the way from Birmingham is a pinch of John Cadbury's chocolate."

From a silver box, she extracted enough small wedges of chocolate for each of us to have one or two.

"May I ask if the sugar came from free laborers?" said Patience as Elizabeth and I stood to help Mandy with supper.

Margery flushed, and Patience said, "Then I cannot partake. Consuming the produce of slaves supports the institution."

Quietly, Margery placed her chocolate wedges back in their gold case.

◊◊◊◊◊◊

My mother-in-law returned with my hungry baby. "Feel free to join the others," said Elizabeth, and I took a corner seat to feed my child.

"Come sit by me," Patience said to Mary Crispin who accepted the invitation by occupying my previous seat. "May I introduce my best friend and most favored confidante, Mary Crispin Ferguson. Some six generations removed, one of her great grandmothers was Rachel Penn, first cousin to William Penn, called somewhat disrespectfully, 'The Founder'."

This was news to me. I found myself smiling at the thought that on her mother's side my child is descended from a Queen Mother and on her father's from the name sake of the state to which my father had hoped to escape. Realizing the latter bordered on the impossible, I asked myself, 'Has Daddy's dream come true? Is he there with Mama even now?' I answered my own question, 'They were sold apart. There is a greater chance that the sun might collide with the moon.'

Margery said, "Although he too was a Quaker, didn't William Penn own slaves?"

The goodwill she had hoped to engender with her chocolate melted almost to the point of evaporation. My mother-in-law turned her gaze on Margery as though she could see the back of the Englishwoman's head. "I answer for Mary Crispin Ferguson alone. Neither I—nor my parents—ever pretended to own others. That is one of the practices introduced by the British, something William Penn called himself. As I understand it, some British Quakers were also slave runners in Africa. On my mother's side there were indentured servants—temporary slaves who themselves owned no others."

I recalled hearing that both my mother-in-law's father and one of her uncles had fought for the Americans in the Revolutionary War. For a time they had renounced their pacifist religion. They had returned to pacifism when it was made clear the false independence did not include those of color. Together with Mary Crispin's assistance with fugitives, and my husband's open flaunting of social restrictions, I judged the family had held onto their spunk.

When the baby had enjoyed her fill, I handed her back to her grandmother and rejoined the kitchen workers. Not long afterwards I peeked in and found that Susan had acted as though she were still hungry and was on Mary Crispin's breast! This was not the first time her grandmother had fed her without asking me, for her own youngest child had yet to be weaned, and more than once it had appeared convenient to wet nurse her granddaughter. But here she was doing so amidst guests, none of whom had given birth themselves, nor do I believe they had imagined a white woman performing an act that tens of thousands of colored women were doing all over the country. I walked over to relieve Mary Crispin who said, "She is content and almost asleep, Sarah. I will burp her and take her back home before supper."

"Please stay," said Patience. "Thee can place her in the crib kept in the library for just such a happy occasion."

"Thank thee for the invitation, but I have my own brood and they would be at sea were it to appear they were motherless."

I kissed my sleeping child's brow, and my mother-in-law left carrying the baby.

"Supper is served," called Mandy leading the way into the formal dining room with Elizabeth and me following.

There was a choice of bean or beef shin soup, followed by mutton, chicken pot pie, peaches in cider, Maryland biscuits, stewed potatoes, boiled cabbage, and parsnips. A balloon pudding, in a white wine sauce, and thin slices of almond cake, topped off the repast.

"On my mother's side, I come from a family of bakers," said Sarah Douglass. "Any one of us would assert the greatness of the oven that baked these biscuits and the tea dainties."

People laughed politely. Douglass may have come from a well-to-do family in the eyes of blacks, but the others were from old money, where usually servants or slaves did the work that earned their fortunes. They were liberal but blind to their privilege.

I could not help surreptitiously watching Margery Barclay eat. Her precision with silverware rivaled that of my professional seamstress mother-in-law with a needle and thread. Moreover, she even chewed her food with studied decorum.

I was still appreciating her when she opened her mouth and said, "I had been led to believe that the dwellings on the frontier were mere hovels, 'log cabins' or 'lean-tos' whatever they might be. London travel guides suggest that they are built to abandon as quickly as a hermit crab leaves behind a shell, but this brick house has a certain…integrity."

I prayed that Patience would put Margery in her place, but she only smiled benevolently and said softly, "My father taught that the wise build to last. Whether it be a ship or a Constitution, flaws should not be a part of the handiwork."

"I was wondering," said Angelina, "Is that a 'widow's walk' above the sleeping floor?"

"I prefer the phrase, 'roof walk'," said Patience.

"A distinction without a difference?" asked Margery.

"I was alone when my father and brothers failed to return," said Patience, "and as an unmarried woman, for whom would I be waiting?"

The room grew quiet until Margery broke the silence by saying, "In my peregrination into the hinterlands of this new country, I have only encountered an occasional savage. Each was unarmed, docile to be blunt. On the whole, rural America is quite quaint, although it cannot be referred to as innocent."

Here was a breathtaking observation. Already America had appropriated the vast majority of acreage from the Atlantic to the Pacific and, I rejected her use of the word "savage." The only piece of her observation with which I could readily agree was the lack of innocence.

I was the youngest present, the only ex-slave, and did not believe that even in Patience Starbuck's home, workers had equal right to speak. Fortunately, Angelina said, "I trust the savages of which thee speaks are the slaveholders."

"I've yet to visit the southlands," said Margery. "Carrying their meager belongings, a Shawnee family came through Cincinnati just as we were preparing to leave. They were quite destitute, as much beggars as any I have seen in London."

"We beggared them, Friend Margery," said Patience. "This very house sits on Caesar's Creek. The namesake was an escaped slave who became a Shawnee and lived to see the theft of all of their ancient homeland."

"Really?" said Sarah Grimké.

"Yes," said Patience. "This house sits on what once was Shawnee land."

"Then you actually have stood face to face with some of these savages?" asked Margery.

"They are not savages," said Patience in a voice that indicated she had tired of playing demure hostess. "The Shawnees are more respectful than most whites I have encountered, and I certainly did not know the ones who, long before my arrival, had been dismissed without compensation. To your implied question, I do count Shawnees among my friends and took it upon myself to travel to Wapakoneta to pay those on that disgraceful reservation for what I believe I can now properly declare my own."

Patience had edges. The Philadelphians silently retreated from the conversation, content to enjoy their first acceptable meal since taking the northern route that was mostly by canal boats and stagecoaches through rough country. Margery was happy to fill the unclaimed space. "I see thy furnishings are by Goddard and Townsend from thy New England home region and that thee uses Waterford Crystal all the way from the center of the civ—, excuse me, the proper world. My Cadbury's chocolate is not the first finery to grace this house."

Patience failed to confirm the obvious or accept the verbal peace offering, leading me to recall my father-in-law's words to a chatterbox child, "Thee should not speak unless the silence will be improved." I longed to see his counsel incorporated, but Margery was of another mind. "I half suspect your shoes are by Clark's."

"I do own a pair from Clark's, but these and most others were made by Sarah's brother, Robin. If I could dream it, he could make it."

"I would love to have a personal shoemaker."

"Although he was not my 'personal shoemaker,' I'd request his company for thee, had he not been kidnapped." Observing that all were finished eating or nearly so, Patience stood abruptly and said, "Our British guest has led us to the subject of this gathering. Shall we retire to the drawing room?"

This room was opposite her parlor, separated only by a magnificent library. Elizabeth and I had been alerted to the plan to use it. We had the chesterfield and single seat chairs arranged so that they appeared to be an amphitheater with Patience's imported chaise lounge the focal point. There was to be no doubt that our hostess would "clerk this meeting." Arm-in-arm, Elizabeth and I settled on the bench in one of her two huge bay windows.

In Quaker style, the meeting began with the settling period of Quaker silence. When she was prepared to speak Patience asked Harriet Beecher, "He has had ample time to consider; will thy father agree to host the anti-slavery meeting?"

"He says it's impossible," said Harriet. "He sounded several key members and it is clear that his board will not countenance it."

"I had thought a Protestant clergyman was nigh on a God," said Margery. Patience gave her such a look that for a time she hushed.

The Philadelphians repositioned themselves. Here was the heart of the reason they had journeyed so far. "No offense intended, Harriet," said Sarah Grimké. "The abolition movement needs no clergymen— hireling or otherwise. They are welcome to join us or go their own way.

Contrary to their high opinion of themselves, the kingdom of heaven can be brought to earth without their cooperation."

"He knows that many women feel that way," said Harriet, "but his hands are tied."

"I counted myself a friend of a Charleston minister," said Angelina. "Earlier he had pastored in New Jersey and although, in private, he criticized slavery, he too felt his hands were tied. I parted company with him when this would-be mentor refused to see that business interests rule this country. It is unreasonable to believe that patient prayer alone will someday free the slaves."

"The great Captain of our salvation will not rest until we are free," said Sarah Douglass suddenly.

"And one day you will be free," said Patience.

"Neither I nor my parents have been enslaved," said Sarah Douglass.

I thought, but did not say, 'Thee is from Africa. So long as one of us is enslaved, thee cannot claim freedom for thyself.'

She continued, "Despite what appears to be scant hope, my poor oppressed brethren and sisters are deserving of similar opportunity. I am not so callous as to believe that standing inches from the fire, I cannot be singed. Even beyond metaphor, along with the enslaved, my complexion demonstrates I *am* singed."

"It may be that the tide is changing just when we most fear being overwhelmed," said Harriet. "Might a deliberate tide wash away an errant flame?"

"I expect that thee is right," said Patience. "If we are willing to be the moon that drives the tide, love may conquer yet."

"Assuming a merciful God," said Sarah Douglass, "He will one day save us. But I expect part of our salvation will be from northern love."

The room grew quiet. Contemplating her words, I found myself warming to this woman. Having grown up among Quakers, she was well aware that members of the Religious Society of Friends are wont to discredit statements made with passion. Tempering her tone, she said in a softer, almost apologetic voice, "There are times when I speak the Truth and leave the consequences to God."

"If thee cannot be thy natural self in my home, I have failed my guests," said Patience.

The meeting continued in areas that were less likely to cause conflict until Margery redirected the conversation to the Grimké sisters, "You two are from the south; is it true that slaveholders view their relations to slaves as no worse than commensal?"

"I'm not certain I understand," said Sarah Grimké.

I held my peace although I too was from the south and fully understood Margery's point. Hard experience had taught me that slaveholders saw no adverse effects to their barbarity. Indeed, they saw themselves as sainted, beyond reproach, and heaven bound with bevies of less than human slaves to wait on them hand and foot in a segregated land beyond pearly gates. On the other hand, along with all other colored people, I was certain that from George Washington and Thomas Jefferson extending to the lowest slaver, Hell awaited them.

"I mean do they feel that their slave holding is inconsequential to the development of their souls?" said Margery.

"Yes," said Angelina, "but that is neither the subject at hand nor is that knowledge likely to free anyone."

"I have been taught," said Margery, "knowledge, although far from free, is freeing. Perhaps thee knows the verse, 'You shall know the Truth, and the Truth shall set you free'."

Patience recaptured the floor, "I have called this gathering because it is my intention to respond to the abomination of '29 when the Cincinnati mob raped, pillaged and drove out over half the city's colored population. Among them was Robin, brother of Sarah

Ferguson here. Recently we learned he was kidnapped by slave catchers and returned to captivity."

"Obviously thee knows such a meeting as this, among those who do not have the right to vote, cannot inspire his return," said Angelina. "What is thy overall purpose for taking a protest to Cincinnati instead of Dayton, which is closer to Waynesville, thus further from the Kentucky brigands who might attack us?"

Her sister said, "My personal goal is simple: to convince our men to remove their feet from the Negro's neck."

"My 'overall' goal is full equality," said Patience. "Soon I intend to apply the freeing medicine of taking Truth into the belly of the whale and harpooning it with gusto. The closer to slave territory, the more noticeable to the demonic terroristic forces."

All of us were surprised by her violent allusion, but she was the daughter of a whaler, a profession that, never shrinking from Leviathan, knows its share of blood.

"Since Lyman Beecher denies us space," continued Patience, "I will convince the Friends in Cincinnati to allow use of the meetinghouse. With righteousness on our side, I will bill it 'Anti-slavery Opposes the Anti-Christians'. Whosoever self-identifies as in opposition may explain their position to the Creator."

Margery found her tongue, "Isn't this a bit more dangerous than necessary? From what I've seen, Americans can be quite crude."

"It is more dangerous to let evil reign," said Sarah Douglass.

"Surely one such as thee would not venture among such race-hating madmen Patience would be inviting to protest?" said Margery.

"Would thee have me remove myself as so many Shawnees here and Lenapes back home have?"

"Their trail of tears was not isolated," said Patience. "The Cincinnati colored refugees who were driven all the way to Canada must not be forgotten."

"From thy anger-filled letters I should have expected that thee would grasp the nettle," said Margery.

"Excuse me?" said Patience.

"Could it be that thy courage borders on bravado?" said Margery.

"I know nothing of courage," said Patience. "My motivation is obedience to The Light. Now, let me hear the concerns of others."

Angelina replied, "If I would never enslave my own child, why should I enslave another's? Common sense shows us that colored women such as Sarah Douglass have ample intellectual capacity, certainly more than Calhoun or Clay or Jackson. That should be a part of thy message."

Patience nodded. "And thee, Sarah Grimké? What weighs on thy spirit in this matter?"

Sarah Grimké answered, "From books I have studied kings and queens. This day, in person, I have studied thee, Patience. Just as there are far more acceptable queens than kings, I have found that thee outstrips most birthright Quaker men I have met."

"It is true that I am birthright, while thee is a convinced Friend," said Patience, "but let me make it clear: Mother died young and I have Father's wind in my sails. He was also birthright. Yes, he, along with my colored nanny, was the one who taught me to be an abolitionist. That said, he was not nearly so radical as is his favorite daughter."

Sarah Grimké said, "But doth thee not think the coloreds would be best served if some voluntarily returned to Africa where they could help their kinsmen find true Christianity? The very fact that so many of them have held onto the faith despite oppression gives evidence of their superior understanding of Christ's message."

"I can judge whether a snowfall was deep or moderate," said Patience. "Measuring the faith of two sets of believers is not in my repertoire. Such people as the Fante are surely as faithful as the best

Christians in this country." She turned to Sarah Douglass, and said, "Friend Sarah Douglass, whether or not thee addresses colonization, another word perchance?"

"Inside I am full, but I will share these things with thee, trusting that I am among friends, none of whom will strive to undercut dreams once expressed."

With the exception of Harriet Beecher, all of the women were Quakers and thus unable to pledge. Quaker word was expected to be good at all times. Seeing no dissenters, Sarah Douglass continued. "I have never dreamed of returning to a place that even my grandparents never saw. I am an American who wants to rally the colored community—both free and enslaved—around education. I envision a mental feast that will call us to actively resist the evil that is American bondage."

"In thy correspondence thee went further," gently prodded Patience.

"Yes, my heart has more," said Sarah Douglass hesitating a moment before saying, almost in a rush, "I envision a bi-racial women's organization whose purpose will be to stand in total opposition to colonization—I have no intention of removing to Sierra Leone or Liberia. I want us to work to abolish slavery in these United States as soon as possible—without any compensation to the slaveholders—and to procure equal civil and religious rights with the white people of this nation."

From a contemplative hush, Patience said, "I have a cousin thee might know, Lucretia Mott."

"I have been in her company but never introduced to her."

"Before thee leaves, I will give a letter of endorsement and she will certainly listen with open heart."

Angelina Grimké said, "Thee stands on holy ground, Sarah Douglass. If thee does not surrender it, back in Philadelphia with this pursuit of improved education for my neighbors I will stand beside thee come flood or fire."

Margery Barclay rediscovered her voice. "We in the British Isles have abolished slavery, but even we have not gone as far as Sarah Douglass suggests."

"Not to join with this vision is to be adrift from the Promised Land," said Patience. Suddenly our hostess turned and looked at me. "Thee is the youngest woman in the room, but if other Sarahs have a word, in my house, I will not have thee, my near neighbor, play Hagar."

"Nor will I be sent muted into a desert," I said. "I encourage thee to take thy message to Cincinnati, not Dayton or Cleveland. Tell them to help my people go free and prevent kidnappers from stealing them."

"Well considered words," said Patience. "Elizabeth, thee has shared so few of thy thoughts. Will thee honor us?"

I squeezed her arm in encouragement. Clear-eyed, my shy sister-in-law said, "There is much to consider, but no reason to hesitate. Forward is the way toward The Light." I smiled and squeezed her arm again.

◊◊◊◊◊◊

The Friends Meeting refused her. Weeks passed before they found hall owners courageous enough to host an abolitionist conference planned by a group of women who did not know their assigned place. Finally, on May Day, Patience staged an anti-slavery conference. The Philadelphians had contented themselves with helping with planning and left via steamship to attend to business at home. My guess is, they were discussing the frontal attack that they themselves would make on the evil institution.

◊◊◊◊◊◊

Elizabeth and I discussed the conference as we sat in the parlor where our illustrious sister had led the consideration of positive change.

"I marvel over the dress Mother made for her," said Elizabeth.

"I watched thy mother make each measurement, cut and stitch. One day I hope to approach her skill."

"Approach? I have reason to believe thee will one day be as fine a seamstress as Mother."

"Really? She is the best in the county."

"Thee could be the best in the state." I was dreaming about such a possibility when Elizabeth shocked me. "In fact, I believe if Patience were not a woman she might be governor or even President."

How could anyone dare to voice such a dream? Women could not even vote let alone run for office. I was saddened beyond words. I knew that side-by-side with Patience's limitations were my own. Some whites would never hire a colored seamstress, few free colored women had the luxury to hire a professional seamstress' services and the vast majority of us were slaves. I said, "Let us pray for a better future."

Patience found us arm-in-arm sitting eyes closed in silence.

◊◊◊◊◊◊

Margery Barclay remained in Cincinnati. She was seated on the dais, back straight and face set as though she ruled the British Empire. Harriet Beecher sat among the small crowd and endured with the rest of us as the male speakers were threatened with tar and feathers and the female speakers were called "He-women," "She-wolves" and "Amazons."

Margery was the third speaker. In clear voice, she apologized for the role the British had played in establishing American slavery. She concluded with her country's present commitment to ending the practice world-wide and her own to press for the expanded use of free trade goods. The time came for the conference hostess to speak. Wearing a dress that I thought of as "violaceous," Patience silently surveyed the room of abolitionists and hecklers. When the mean-spirited finally quieted she said, "I am impatient Patience. May the world know the slaves not only deserve freedom, but also that I will do all in my power to see to their freedom. If some find this idea too much to bear, I suggest they remove to Russia and apply for the job of serf. Let our people go. If not, instead of a flood, one day this land may be cursed with fire."

How I wished I had possessed the courage and standing to be a speaker, but at 18 and holding a forged free paper, it was not my turn to shine. I promised myself, one day the world will know I am here.

KENTUCKY DRUMS: A FANTASY

I often regret not listening to tales my Fante-born mother told me about the old country. In her natural voice she would tell stories that hinted of magic, something my father called "superstition." What could a Virginia born child slave make of such a world view? In partial penance, I am going to relate the following story as closely as possible to the way my Afro-Shawnee friend, Caesar told it. Like the Fante, the Shawnee way of seeing the world is so different that I simply say, "It is a mystery."

Coming down from Ohio into Kentucky, Caesar recalled the buffalo trace that had run through the heart of Shawnee country. They had disappeared from the area south of what had become Columbus, Ohio and north of Cumberland River. Before the whites arrived, this throughway was Shawnee and Cherokee patriots north-south route and had taken the name "Warrior's Trail." The tide of white invasion was not stemmed. On, this late spring morning of 1832, nearly all Shawnee warriors were either dead or on reservations, the Cherokee were preparing for removal and the road was paved.

At age 40, the retired Shawnee warrior was on a mission of peace. He drove a fine coach holding Patience Starbuck, a wealthy Quaker woman, and me, a runaway pretending to be her slave. At the coach's rear rode my brother, Dan, also in the guise of a slave. The four of us were intent on finding and purchasing the freedom of a third sibling, kidnapped and sold into slavery by Bacon Tate, a white man whose assistants included a colored man named Naphtali Long.

The land ripened before our eyes. More and more butterflies worked among yellow buttercups and variously shaded wild roses. Moving southward, warmer temperatures, greater moisture, and less cloud cover caused summer to seem one day nearer in the lushness of vegetation and fat abundance of animals, for every 20 or so miles the coach traveled—almost exactly its best pace per hour. Seated atop the coach, Caesar smiled at the ripening beauty. Holding the reins with one hand, he lifted his water pouch from under the bench and savored the special sweetness of Kentucky springs.

The weather called for a breech cloth and moccasins, yet he was dressed in full-length white shirt, stockings and knee-length pants; navy blue double-breasted coat with tails; and high-top black boots. A high, cylindrical, patent leather hat sat on the seat beside him, reserved for stationary periods.

Just north of Boonesborough, Caesar glimpsed the vision of a panther amidst high grasses. Was it the spirit of Tecumseh? Soon afterwards he heard Shawnee drumming. African drums joined with the Shawnee. The message was unmistakable: some evil threatened his people, Shawnee and African. He was called to confront it.

Caesar flexed his right foot in its boot, feeling his free paper—a passport bearing the family's first surname, "Smith." A century earlier, a Shawnee war party had rescued one of his great grandfathers from slavery. Once adopted, that grandfather and every one of his descendants married another Shawnee. Like that ancestor, Caesar also worked as an interpreter; but he'd won most of his reputation as a young warrior, under Tecumseh, who had died in battle almost 20 years earlier, then as an Underground Railroad conductor.

Coming over a rise, Caesar saw two boys duck into high grasses a quarter mile away. He kept a steady pace. About the time those boys must have thought themselves safe, he halted the coach and said in a low voice, "Stand up and talk!" He leapt to the ground. "If you're running away, I'm your friend. I've helped hundreds just like you in my time."

They rose slowly and the older boy said, "We got our free papers."

"And we aim to stay free," said the younger.

"And you better watch out, Mister," said the elder. "Over in Richmond, Orville Clay and his friends getting ready to lynch a man named Pete Jeffers. Mr. Clay saying Pete disrespected his wife, Miss Clay."

The mention of lynching frightened me so that I looked toward Patience, the nearest adult. She came from a Nantucket whaling family and had the proper skin color. What had she to fear? She motioned for me to calm myself.

"Sir," said the younger. "You hear all them drums?"

"Don't worry," said Caesar. "The drummers won't hurt you. They're the ghosts of warriors long dead."

Maybe the boys would have said more, but fleeing the ghosts seemed wiser.

Caesar drove the coach onward to a Boonesborough inn. There, he said to the three people with him, "Stay here for a while. I'm going to take a horse and see what's happening over in Richmond."

Patience let Dan help her down from the coach and led me into the inn where I helped her undress before going to the out building reserved for female slaves. Meanwhile, under guard, Dan cared for the horses and was led to the building where male slaves were kept under lock and key. Caesar displayed his free paper but was told, "That won't get you no closer to a bed inside the inn than that nigger slave."

Caesar's dark skin would be even more conspicuous if he wore either his Shawnee clothing or a slave's rags. He put on the outfit white men preferred for freed men: oversized overalls, baggy calico shirt, and cheap brogans. Still hanging from his neck, hidden under his shirt, was the small doeskin pouch he never took off: the lone sign of his Shawnee heritage. It held a lock of his wife's hair, reminding him of love's possibilities and two panther claws once taken off a fool, reminding him of the limits of courage.

Well hidden in his new costume were three knives, a pistol, and a tomahawk. He knocked twice and was let out of the slave quarters.

Upon release, he was told, "If you ain't back by the midnight bell, boy, you'll sleep in the briars. Davy Ray will be on night shift and ain't the kinda man to break the Captain's rules."

◊◊◊◊◊◊

Near dusk Caesar arrived at the lynching site in Richmond. Two hundred white men, women and children gathered around massive bonfires, drinking whiskey from kegs stamped with the name Pete Jeffers, smoking tobacco aged on nearby farms, and ignoring the nervous barefoot slaves who tended to the meat roasting at the fires. The slave chefs and cleaning staff heard the African drumming and then looked about to see where it came from. The heavily chained condemned man prayed as he sat between two armed guards who like the other whites heard only their own good cheer.

Caesar avoided the crowd and looked around. He came upon a colored man intently watching the party lights. The man held a plank in one hand, a hog butchering knife in the other. Landing on the balls of his feet, Caesar dismounted in one smooth jump.

"My friend—"

The man dropped his plank and ducked his head. Then he took in Caesar's dress, face and the African cadences of his voice. "Man, is you crazy? Don't be coming up on somebody like that!"

"Where's the families and other scouts?"

A stranger was a suspect in a state where only two in a hundred of the colored population was free: Caesar might be an errand boy for those planning the lynching. "I don't know you or what you talking about. I'm just minding my business."

"And here I mistook you for a hero. Where are the other lookouts and the ones you're trying to protect?"

Caesar had a way of growling, low and powerfully, when patience was no longer a virtue. It tended to compel truthful answers. "There," the scout said, pointing out two men across the square, watching the mob.

"And the families? How many are there?"

"Only six free families in this town. We all live by the little runoff on the west side."

"Your name?"

"Ezra."

"All right, Ezra—I'll get the families. I'm Caesar. Like you I'm colored, but I'm a Shawnee warrior too. Get the other lookouts and meet me out where the old Indian village used to be. Gather whatever horses and wagons you can."

Caesar rode to Richmond's colored section. At the house furthest from the bonfires he knocked at a blockaded door. "Hey there inside! I'm a friend come to help."

He waited. Finally, a woman called out, "How I know I can trust you?"

"Did I set fire to the house?"

From inside came the noise of shifting furniture. She opened the door. Caesar saw three trembling, small children, blanketed in a corner. Their mother said, "My big boys is hiding elsewhere."

"Gather these babies, and let's go."

Caesar heard someone coming and reached for his tomahawk.

The man whose bulk filled the doorway saw the upraised weapon and said, blustering, "Jane—this man molesting you?" The man took another bite of the pig foot he held. Jane looked on her husband with contempt and hurried the children out past him. He redirected to Caesar, "This is my house. You heard of me, Naphtali Long?"

By reputation, yes; Caesar knew Naphtali as an employee of white bounty hunters who captured not only runaways but free men as well. "I know the name," Caesar said. Naphtali stood a bit taller. "But name and reputation won't save you if the white folks here get riled. I've seen five men lynched, but 17 colored folk killed in the final count. You better help me high tail these people outta here, before that mob ends up raping and killing everybody here, you included."

Some of the white men who planned to string up his neighbor Pete Jeffers were Naphtali's fellow bounty hunters, but he too had seen how far the killing spirit could go, once unleashed. And he suspected that a few wouldn't mind the chance to kill a turncoat.

"Just so you know, Naphtali, I'm Caesar. If you come with us, you'll do what I say. But I look out for even shiftless polecats like you."

Naphtali struggled to mask his fear when an elderly slave with stiffly starched red headscarf came through the door, rudely shoving him aside.

"Is you finished talkin' to this fool?" said the tobacco-chewing elder. She spat a dark stream through the doorway, then said, "You the nigger Injun Ezra told me about?"

"My ancestors were African and Shawnee."

"Ain't that what I just said? Shawnees supposed to be scarier than cholera, so how about you puttin' a hurt on the folk out there at the lynchin'?"

"One Shawnee against one hundred Kentucky rifles?"

"In your life I bet you done scalped ninety-eleven folk; I need some revenge."

91

"Ain't no point in revenge."

She lowered the thin and knobby finger pointed at him. "Well, if you ain't got no more sense than to guard the unwanted, is there any Shawnee nearby that might help a old lady?"

Caesar considered. "I know a woman who might help you," he said. "About a half mile out of town the road forks; keep on straight and soon you'll hear a small waterfall. Turn downstream 'til you see a big boulder. Offer some tobacco at the rock. Take 10 more steps…make that 12 steps. Turn to the right and keep on 'til you smell honeysuckle. Behind those bushes is the opening to a cave. I have to stoop; you won't."

"I might be short, but I'm full grown, son. Power ain't measured in inches."

"No, ma'am," Caesar said. As she turned, he said, "Don't get lost."

"If a pup can point it, a woman can find it."

Caesar chuckled as she left. Meanwhile Naphtali licked the pig foot grease remnants from his hands and dried them on his pants. "I thought you was in such a rush to leave," he said to Caesar. "For once that stupid slave Nellie was right."

Caesar crowded past him, out of the house, heading to where Ezra and the others gathered. Among the refugees, Caesar said to Ezra, "This man Pete have kin?"

"Mattie over there."

Caesar rode up to her wagon. "A shame what they're doing. I'm sorry, Ma'am."

Mattie lifted her head and pushed back a woolen hood, revealing a long slim neck and hair like lamb's wool. "I loved Pete, but he never shoulda been drinking with them white folks, nor said nothing about Miss Cindy, either. Just because she was in her Sunday dress didn't make her nothing special."

"You're right; but for your family's sake, don't blame Pete for their wrongs."

"All thirty-nine are here," said Ezra.

"Mattie," said Caesar, "keep just behind me, all right? Jane, your wagon next."

"Ain't you going to wait on my big boys?" Jane called.

"They ain't in the count," said Ezra. "I seen them two high-tailing it earlier this afternoon."

Jane shook her head sadly. "The preacher said they'd end up shiftless like their pa."

"Woman, I'm right here!" said Naphtali.

"That's supposed to bring me happiness?" said Jane. "I wish somebody would kidnap and sell your sorry ole self."

"All right, y'all," said Caesar. "Screaming at each other won't help us get away."

"Are you telling me I can't talk in my own hometown?" said Naphtali.

"Naphtali, a man who'd track down his own wife's cousin is worse than worthless. And I'm the peace chief of this village. Those without feathers don't sit on the Council."

◊◊◊◊◊◊

Later grumbling, Nellie admitted to Caesar that she had ignored his directions and followed the sound of the drums. The source of the music seemed to lie deep within the cave. Near its entrance she found a woman eating a bowl of venison stew. Even before speaking, Nellie offered a gift basket. The woman stood to accept it. As they sat together, Nellie noted the woman's deeply lined face, buckskin dress, and glints of firelight on her silver necklace and earrings.

The hostess said, "I've never seen a weave like this basket."

"And unless you know somebody else Fante you won't ever again."

"Because my spirit walks always with Caesar, I knew you were coming."

"I'm a drum-callin' somebody too. As loud as y'all's drums playin', you shoulda figured somebody'd show up."

"You are honored; normally only the Grandmother's children hear Shawnee drums."

Nellie considered but rejected the idea of allowing her to hear the Fante drums. By the fire's light, she scanned the cave: bowls and eating utensils; baskets of seasoning herbs and dried meat; buffalo robes and animal skins; wood piles; a bow and arrows, numerous spears and a tomahawk.

"You expectin' trouble?"

"Always." The hostess rose to hobble over to her extra bowls.

Nellie spied two passageways extending further back into darkness. On returning, the hostess noticed Nellie's searching eyes. Without commenting, she ladled food for her guest.

"How'd you know I'm hongry?" Nellie said.

Autumn Turtle guffawed. "An old nosy woman who travels through strange woods is sure to work up a hunger."

Nellie swallowed her reflexive ire. "This stew's tasty enough; I guess I can stand a little smart talk, Miss Ma'am. They calls me Nellie, but my real name is Nane. How some fool came to the idea Nane sounds like Nellie is beyond me."

"I am Autumn Turtle. Exactly what brings you here, Nane? Tell it simple and quick."

"There's trouble in Richmond, and I'm tired of gettin' my rump kicked. I want to kick back."

"I know the place. Years ago, at the Battle of the Thames, their mayor killed and scalped the father of my great nephew, Stalking Panther—Caesar, to you."

"One dead man don't stop the carnival," said Nane waiting for a response that never came. "It unsettles my stomach to sit idly by while the white folks lynch Pete Jeffers," said Nane. "My mama and her mama both was best hand woman to the Queen Mother of Fante-land. I weren't born to be weak."

"When my spirit learned from Caesar that a man would be lynched, I moved the heart of my great grandson. John Fairchild is on his way."

"Fairchild? 'The baddest white man in Kentucky' is one of y'all Injuns?"

"You cannot judge a man by his color; many around here have Shawnee blood."

"The masters call Fairchild 'wild'."

"About that, they're right."

"But what if he comes too late?"

"That's why I let you hear our drums. Between us, maybe we can make another way."

Now Nane spoke more humbly than she had before. "They took me from Fante-land before I got finished with my trainin'. All I got is a touch of motherland trainin' and what I picked up on my own. But you know how to snatch somebody's thinkin', don't you?"

"Yes, Shawnee thinking, as you 'snatch' coloreds'. Through the power of fire and smoke surrounded by stone, my spirit walks where it wishes." Autumn Turtle paused and lit a pipe. "Juju ladies without African root medicine find a way. So have I."

The cave was full of ancestral ghost sighs. Their shadows danced on walls. Hedged all around its sanctuary was the forest's living spirit. Nane nodded once, sharply. "This is a good place," she said. "I can do my work here. Let's get to makin' some bad people hurt."

"Our spirits together can do things we could not do alone. But let's use compassion to find justice—"

"Compassion? Now there's a mighty big word. What's it mean?"

"Feeling sorry for people who fall short."

"Now why would I want to waste 'compassion' on folk who love shortchangin'? I'm just an old lady ready to make the wrong do right. But it's your place; we'll try it your way."

Nane and Autumn Turtle looked into the visions of the fire together. Soon they touched the First Mind.

When Caesar spoke of "First Mind" I recalled my mother saying, "First Mind say ain't nothin' about Fruits of the Spirit got a bit of good except us slaves."

My father had said, "Esi, no one can be perfectly evil."

Although she rarely disagreed with her husband while in front of their children she said, "You talkin' 'bout what you hope. I'm talkin' about what I know."

◊◊◊◊◊◊

Orville Clay took another swig of Pete Jeffers Whiskey and, wiped his upper lip, and said, "I knew when Naphtali stole Pete's recipe, we'd be home free." There were nods all around from his friends.

"Yep," said a man named Bacon Tate, "Naphtali's about as good a nigger as I ever knew."

One matriarch smoked calmly, the other chewed tobacco as if it were cud, Autumn Turtle and Nane peered into the cave's fire and smoke. They saw Cindy push a blond lock from her eyes and wipe away tears. "Orville honey," she said, trying to smile sweetly. "I really wasn't insulted by what the nigger said. I took it as a compliment."

"It's about honor, Cindy. Just like I couldn't live without you, I couldn't live with you shamed. What if niggers could compliment any blue-eyed beauty they wanted? What next?"

Soon after they were married, Orville had broken Cindy's nose with a backhand and then claimed it would regain its original shape once healed. In this, he had proven a false prophet. And yet she forgave him numerous private slappings because publicly he acted as though he worshipped her. The abuse felt worth the pedestal.

"Honey, if you let Pete go at noon tomorrow, that'll be warning enough. He'll get the scare of his life and won't even think of speaking out of turn to his betters again."

"That ain't the issue, and I don't need no woman's preaching. Look at all these folks enjoying themselves. They can see a scared nigger anytime; they want one hanged."

When Caesar related that Nane had reported this conversation I was so outraged that I used profanity, something Patience had never heard from my mouth. She said, "Why Sarah, hast thee never heard this hateful word."

I said, "I cannot count the times I've heard it and worse. That does not mean I've grown accustomed to being disrespected."

◊◊◊◊◊◊

The first time Autumn Turtle touched John Fairchild's spirit, he was already one of the age's most controversial men: a presumed white Kentucky abolitionist befriended by Caesar, Levi Coffin, and many others sympathetic to the cause of the colored people. One of Fairchild's great grandfathers had arrived in America indentured to a rich plantation owner. He'd run away; been recaptured by bounty hunters, whipped, branded and had the remaining time of his indenture doubled. A dozen years later, finally freed, that ancestor had married a Shawnee. Fairchild knew the story back to front. The hardships of that ancestor were the inspiration of all his good works.

When Autumn Turtle alerted Fairchild of the imminent lynching in Richmond, he gathered a seven-man citizens' cavalry of like-minded white men who would have charged with him into a stone wall or off a cliff. They too despised the big slaveholders who kept poor whites in destitution by forcing them to compete with unpaid laborers. It was also common knowledge that all lynchings were approved by the upper classes. Any mission that opposed the wealthy had these men's support.

By the time Fairchild and his friends arrived in Richmond, they found Pete Jeffers already dead, hanging from a willow. The victim's murderers had planned to let him swing until bit by bit he was picked apart or fell to earth. Fairchild led his men, furious and frustrated, into the general store, and pulled shotguns on the customers, Richmond's mayor, among them. The citizens' cavalry ordered Pete buried under the lynching tree.

Word spread: "Some strangers are burying the nigger right in the town square."

The mayor was compelled to set an example. Shovel in hand, he led the others outside.

Taking off his new shoes and socks, he dug so fast drops of sweat fell from his brow. The storeowner said, "Even niggers don't work that hard! Damn, Your Honor, my wife said you was there too at the—"

Fairchild turned his attention to the storeowner. The man shut his mouth.

The mayor collapsed from exhaustion. While he was being carried away, the husband who claimed his wife had been dishonored arrived.

"What's going on here?" Orville demanded. "Just what right do you have to do this?"

Fairchild lifted the barrel of his shotgun. "I wondered the same thing about you."

No one volunteered an answer and Fairchild removed his hat. His men followed suit. "Let us pray," Fairchild said, over the grave. "Lord, take this man into the bosom of Abraham. Protect his kinfolk and everybody who knew him. As for the rascals who lynched him, may they burn in Hell. Amen."

Fairchild looked around to see whether anyone felt like challenging the petition; no one did. He and his men slowly rode away.

◊◊◊◊◊◊

Caesar knew from stories that the road to Eskippakaithiki was once a busy route to Kentucky's major Shawnee village. Now a rarely used path, it ran almost invisibly through high wiry weeds, and led to the abandoned site from which the state's name derived. It amazes me how often the conquerors mispronounce original names and even when their mistakes are pointed out, they refuse to correct themselves.

During the refugees' flight from Richmond, the beats of the Shawnee drumming changed, and the African drumming became more polyrhythmic. A child of both cultures, Caesar could distinguish easily between the two. But few of the fleeing were familiar with drums, as it was a capital offense for coloreds to own or play them in Kentucky. What the spirits intended as solace proved unsettling to the refugees. Small children clung to their mothers and older siblings; men cloaked unease with bravado; women set their faces against whatever would come next.

"Stop sniveling," Jane told her children. "Y'all the worst-behaved kids out here! Drums don't hurt people."

By first light the Richmond families had trekked eight miles, reaching the outskirts of Eskippakaithiki. "I know you're all tired," said Caesar, "but the wagons can't make it over this ground. We got to walk from here. This last little bit is through swamp."

They left the wagons and put the horses on leads. Soon after setting out again, Naphtali said, "You see them rattlers?"

Ezra said without even looking around, "Fool! Snakes don't bite nobody but the Devil's children."

Naphtali pushed his way to the front. Panting for breath, he said to Caesar, "Them drums about to make us lose our mind. You the high and mighty Shawnee, why don't you do something about it?"

"I can't even make you shut up; so how do you expect me to stop drums coming from the other world?"

Dawn broke while the refugees crossed the swamp. A full-throated scream ripped the air. Caesar halted the line and hurried back, reassuring the terrified people. Midway down the line, he came upon Naphtali sprawled across the path, legs in the mire.

"I'd swear on my mama's grave 'twern't no snakes," said Ezra.

Caesar examined the corpse and said, "There are no fang marks."

Mattie crowded in for a good look and said. "I guess his heart gave out."

Naphtali's wife, Jane, stopped nursing and readjusted her dress. "That fool's heart gave out years ago," she said. "He done kidnapped 287 colored folk by his own count. By mine, he done caught my cousin and ruint both my big boys. Will somebody hold this baby? I need to pry them rings off his hands before we push him in. Like as not he stole every one of them rings."

Rings collected, Jane rifled his pockets, extracting cash and a worthless piece of paper with the words "Pete's Whiskey" scrawled across the top. The illiterate woman tossed it onto the muck and continued searching. "Hey, Ezra? You want these boots and shirt before I shove him off?"

I doubt that this was common practice from whoever her people were in Africa but from the legends I have heard about Naphtali Long, whether this was the original or someone who made up the composite treasonous man, he deserved such treatment.

◊◊◊◊◊◊

"Well, I did it," Nane said. "Nyame knows, I tried for years—at last I gave Naphtali a conscience."

"It took two," said Autumn Turtle, "but the knowledge of what he'd done struck him down."

"Well." Nane shrugged. "Jane's the only kin I got left. Before Orville could sell her, I bought my grandbaby's freedom with 40 years of vegetable garden money, then gave her more to start out. But she up and married Naphtali. That idjit snatched my money from her like it was his'n! Woulda done her better startin' cold like I did. Later on, Naphtali—" Throughout Nane's diatribe, Autumn Turtle abided in silence. "Now a conscience for that uppity Cindy Clay. I nursed her grandpa, midwifed her mama, and cleaned up after her from baby 'til just yesterday. Once I loved that girl like she was mine. Then last week Orville hit her again. Because I seen it, she had the nerve to slap *me*! Let's give that heifer a peek at right and see what happens when she learns some sense."

◊◊◊◊◊◊

When Mrs. Orville Clay slid the emergency rope beneath her shawl, only a slave saw her. She was in no position to say, "Stop thief!" The entire affair shamed Cindy like a child caught stealing cookies. She set off for a spot that had been her childhood retreat.

Her favorite tree extended above the cliff's edge. One of the lower boughs seemed sturdy enough to bear her weight. With a steady hand she tossed the rope once, twice. Third time was the charm.

A tear glistened in Nane's left eye; she'd raised this girl.

A fallen branch helped Cindy nudge the noose to the best position. The sun had risen brightly, and her heart beat like a drum. Cindy placed the loop over her head and pinned her final message onto her dress. "There was another way."

◊◊◊◊◊◊

When I read this to my family I was asked if any part of it was from my imagination. Who knows? When I read my transcription to

Caesar he said, "I am an interpreter of Indian languages and the white man's. You have interpreted what I witnessed. That makes us equals."

MOUNTAIN CLIMBING

I felt comfortable knowing the famous abolitionist, Patience Starbuck, led our four-member rescue mission in search of my kidnapped brother. We, arrived in Friendsville, Tennessee, a Quaker colony established in 1795, the year of my parents' capture in Fante-land. The locals were active in the abolition movement and every year since 1787 Tennessee Quakers, had petitioned the state legislature to free the slaves. They also had befriended the Cherokees. Of course, they became favorites with scores of free colored people who had settled in the area as well as the indigenous people, who, in 1832, were in the process of being dispossessed of their homeland.

A cousin of Patience's invited us to sleep in beds and, I hoped, lay down our drama, including the lynching we had come upon just weeks earlier. Only the women accepted beds.

Caesar, was our group's coach driver and guide, culturally he was of Shawnee, Cherokee, Creek and African descent. However, he was more to me: He had guided me and two of my brothers when, at age 13, I had fled slavery. Since that time, effectively he had been my father. As soon as the horses were cared for, he went off to explore the area that once relatives had called their homeland. My brother, Dan, who, like me, pretended to be Patience's slave, claimed he would be most comfortable sleeping in a bedroll under the coach.

On the second day of our stay, in the midst of three days of rain,

Sam Houston, once governor of Tennessee and future President of Texas, came to visit a Friendsville merchant. He had only recently left President Andrew Jackson's slave plantation, the Hermitage, and although he was in self-inflicted exile, was feeling good about his next major move. With him was his tall, slim, wife, a Cherokee who had been born Tiana Rodgers. Tiana was so breathtakingly beautiful that she was the only woman I had ever met whose loveliness compared to Esi, my mother.

Patience had a male cousin arrange afternoon tea at the house where we were being hosted. When she invited me to tea with her and the Houstons, I said, "Will Sam Houston be attending?" I was told he would. I said, "As one who was born a slave, to sit as an equal with a member of the slave holding class has long been my dream."

The 6'6" legend arrived with several white feathers in his long-braided hair and wearing an embroidered white doeskin shirt covered in beads. Beneath the shirt were traditional deerskin leggings. Tiana, the braider of his hair and maker of his clothing, wore a long blue dress covered in shells and metal trinkets, some of which were silver. Her dancing eyes missed nothing.

Houston had barely touched his first cup of tea when Patience said, "What if I told you this nation is heading toward Civil War?"

He smiled. "On such occasion I would gratify you by explaining, there will be no war."

"And if there is?" Patience asked.

"Ma'am, no differences can arise between myself and myself," said Houston laughing.

"Excuse me?"

"If I've learned anything about myself I know I'll not fight uphill," said Houston. "I've already had occasion to think of suicide and chose life."

"That speaks well of thee," said Patience, "but what of thy friends?"

"I'm afraid, ma'am, that there's a class of noisy second-rate men lusting for *all* of this country, but they are not friends of mine. I stand very much alone as the Cherokee advocate."

"Surely thee did not think I meant a Civil War over or against the Indians! Although for eons this land was all theirs, as we speak the Native Americans are not even considered a part of this country."

"I know civil wars happened in England and France, but those of us in Dixie would never be so foolish as to rebel, ma'am. The north has more money, metal, and men. If it could not cannonball us out of existence, it would starve us to death. George Washington and Thomas Jefferson knew this. That's why they tricked Adams and the others into allowing for slaves while still speaking of liberty and justice for all. I repeat, there will be no war."

"I see thee in full Indian regalia but have heard that thee participated in the desecration of the Creeks at a place called Horseshoe Bend," said Patience.

"Have you ever regretted a youthful mistake?"

Patience turned red.

"Forgive my lapse of manners ma'am. I was almost killed by more than a summer ague or simple fatigue in that battle—smashed shoulder, broken arm, barbed arrow in my leg."

"My heart bleeds for the wounds of an invader set on annihilation, but that does not speak to my concern."

"If I may continue, so that I might reach my central point." He waited for an apology that Patience did not offer. "After the battle I was unable to move, but to be most clear, regrettably the Creeks fought with ferocity, refusing to surrender. Just like in scalping, the men who stripped their skin below the waist and made bridle reins for the dragoons and boot legs for the infantry, were honoring Creek courage. The few survivors understood this. There was no desecration, only me wishing I had been anywhere other than on that killing field."

"All barbarism is appalling: what of the cutting off of noses?" asked Patience.

"Except for the fact I was too wounded to participate, you are well informed for a northern woman."

"I have a dear friend who was one of the survivors."

"I can assure you that General Jackson ordered a simple nose count. War is not for the faint of heart. That was past history. Now, in present history, I am Raven, a Cherokee not a Creek, just as the King of England is a Brit, not a Frenchman."

"Can these Cherokees trust thee, Sam Houston?"

"They'll never be mistreated by me. I'm a law-abiding man who has often traveled to Washington on their behalf. As you noted, it's true that in my youth I fought some cantankerous red men to the death; now if they find solace, it may well be owing to my love for them. I'm also drawn to leadership, a man who rose from ensign to lieutenant to colonel to governor. I subscribe to the belief that a leader improves the life of all who live under his governance. The good shepherd uses his rod not to beat but to guide, not to annihilate but to keep in line."

"Of the Indians that I have known," said Patience, "not one struck me as sheep-like."

Houston paternally smiled. "I regret that I had only six months of education. I'm not a man of many words. I've spoken more words this afternoon than the Lord usually rations me in a week."

My youth was spent as a slave where I was trained to surreptitiously watch the eyes of the powerful. Although she never contributed to the conversation, what I saw in the eyes of Houston's wife, Tiana, seemed to indicate that in presenting himself as a gallant, he had overstated his case. I also recognized that, even though his head faced away from her, she had signaled him to put up the white flag that was his final statement.

Houston excused himself claiming he needed to buy a new gun.

◊◊◊◊◊◊

After the dishes were cleaned and put away in cupboards, I found myself alone with Tiana. Away from her husband, Tiana's words flowed as though at tea someone had deliberately dammed them. "Escaping parlor talk is like finding a cool breeze on a hot day," she began. "I and my people were talked about without me ever being asked for my opinion. Most whites have a way of discussing the fate of others as though those with different skin tones are without minds." I said nothing. "Even sadder, they have no understanding of democracy. Although your mistress speaks bluntly, I'm told among their men, nearly all white women have no say in decision making. This is not the Cherokee way. We always are consulted, and sometimes we stand apart and prevent their actions."

"You are blessed," I said simply.

"You seem to be free," she observed. I pretended to understand Tiana's words as a reference to me having no present responsibilities, and she continued. "With the break in the rain, let us take a walk. Being cooped up stunts growth. I would like to share your company, hear your voice."

I waited as she picked up a light blanket that she draped across an arm. Like the child I had long outgrown, I fell behind her, following the older woman's lead. She stopped, smiled, and took my hand. I stepped up beside her.

"My husband has told me that behind every successful man there is a great woman. He has never explained why she does not walk beside him or what value there is in a woman being obscured. Without anyone trying to control us, you and I are free to be equals on this walk."

We walked in tandem although we both recognized it was her country and who lead through parts unknown. We had talked for only a few minutes when I said, "Your English is as good as mine."

"I was thinking the same thing. You use yours like a skilled woman with a knife," said Tiana.

"My father thought English was a key to Freedom," I answered.

"Was he right?"

"I've always known the language, but I've never entered a place called Freedom." I waited for a response; none came. "How," I continued, "did you learn *your* English?"

"Among my ancestors are whites along with Cherokees and Shawnees."

"But I thought you were pure Cherokee," I said.

"I am pure Cherokee. People cannot be less than pure—I'm *living* as a Cherokee."

I of all people knew that purity is a matter of behavior, but there was a divergence in world views. As a black woman, although my husband was a white man, regardless of the context, I remained forever black.

"Then your husband is Cherokee?" I asked.

"For now," said Tiana. "A few years ago, he was the white governor of stolen land now mispronounced as Tennessee. Before then he was Cherokee. Before then he was a white dreamer. What he'll be a few years from now, the Great Spirit will determine."

"With help from him," I said, boldly.

Tiana laughed, "The more he refuses to listen, the more 'help' he will be giving the One who always knows what is right."

We walked a great distance as I pondered her words. I broke the silence. "Isn't it odd that a former governor lives among the Cherokees?"

"Long before the first time my husband lived with the Cherokees, the Quaker, Joseph McMinn, lived among us," explained Tiana.

"Patience has spoken of him. She said McMinn came from Free Quakers."

"Are there slave Quakers?"

"If so I haven't met them," I said, not disclosing that I considered myself both a Quaker and free—although my free paper was a forged passport. "Some Free Quakers left the majority and fought in the Revolutionary War."

"Ahh!" cried Tiana. "The war they sometimes call 'for Independence'. During and after that war, millions of acres were stolen from my *independent* people: same war, different views."

"And those same treasonous people to the British continue to keep millions of my stolen people as far away from independence and the pursuit of happiness as they can.

"Every black person I have met, even those who have never learned to read, knows the word, 'hypocrite'."

"We too know that word. It is a useful word for these times. Seeing so many self-righteous lies told must help our people learn the word's meaning."

"Yes."

"Joseph McMinn also went on to become governor of Tennessee, where he supported both stealing our land and slavery," said Tiana. "Hundreds of whites and Negroes have become Cherokees. Those who returned to their birth people seldom remember the love and respect we gave them."

"Much of this is new to me," I said. "I've not traveled much. I've not seen a single Indian village, but it seems strange that others would run away to join you; from everything I've seen and heard, most Americans act as though they hate you as much as they hate us."

"The whites are great imitators, Sarah. If they see something good—which usually means where they can make money—many will try to join it. Some of them will even try to take it over. There is much to like about the Cherokees. We don't beat our own. We rarely go hungry. We don't allow some to lord it over others. We give warriors more chances to raid, but our wars are rarely long. We don't assign men to state capitals and Washington where day after day, year after year, they are expected to make law after law, taking away freedom after freedom. Much of what I say, I've heard my husband say, but I think there's another reason for joining us that he does not talk about."

"What's that?"

"My husband has said Cherokee women are much prettier, but I've seen other women, and I don't believe we stand that far above them." I looked at her face and it seemed to have grown even more beautiful since the hour I had first set eyes on her.

She continued, "I do know that we find less reason to hide who we are inside while loud men lord it over us, and in the heat, away from leering white eyes, we wear fewer clothes." We laughed together.

"My mother taught us that in her homeland the Fante wore few clothes," I said.

"Did she give you any other keys to freedom, which you have already said is not to be found in white speech?"

"I'm afraid because I was not interested in Africa, I don't know much about it."

"That is an irreparable loss." She paused. "Returning to whites imitating our nations, they come to the frontier uninvited. This is true even of the Quakers whose company we enjoy today. As an uninvited guest, whatever respect any white gives, they are a part of the problem. They are destroying our way of life just by being here. What's more, they obviously don't care."

"I was told Tecumseh once said that. Therefore, it sounds very Shawnee."

"I am a Shawnee," said Tiana.

"Who lives Cherokee," I said with a smile.

She laughed. "Sometimes against their women's counsel, the

warriors of the various bands of Shawnees and Cherokees have fought each other as well as for and against the whites, but I am not at odds with the parts of myself. Are you?"

What could I say? I was the child of a captive Fante and a rapist slaveholder. Mother despised him and he was obsessed with her. Tiana did not push for an answer. As I have never seen a new friend do, she reached out and touched me. Her fingers did not squeeze my arm but they were as powerful as any slave's I have known. We continued our walk.

◊◊◊◊◊◊

Wildflowers were everywhere. I often filled lulls in the conversation with short forays to pick blanket flowers, clasping coneflowers, or yellow cosmos. Usually I merely examined them, twirled them and placed one in the pocket of my apron. Once, instead, I placed a flower behind an ear and pirouetted in the sunny breeze as if I were a child or a woman alone. Tiana let me be myself, never making me feel like she indulged me.

We had walked and talked for miles when in the distance I saw a group of black-eyed Susans. I redirected my gaze, trying to still my heart. I skipped over and smelled the flowers, but did not pick any.

Tiana smiled and said, "Sam Houston is not my first husband."

"Does that bother you?" I asked.

"Why should it? This is not my first dress, and I am not bothered."

"Why'd you tell me this? I was not taught to question what happens between a woman and a man."

"I've watched your face, and I can tell you're separated from your first husband."

"Is it that clear?"

"And there are children, at least a girl. I'd wager her name is Susan," said Tiana.

I was astonished. "Yes, I have a single child, and her name is Susan."

"Ohio, did you say? You travel far for an American woman who feels ties."

I answered the implied question. "I'm searching for my stolen brother."

"A brother is not like a husband." She turned and pointed. "Do you see that far peak?"

"Which one?"

"You chose the right answer. There are two standing side by side. Either 'Yes' or 'No' would have satisfied me. One is a brother and one is a sister. I and my people have climbed both many times. Sometimes we look for game or plants, medicine or material for weapons, peace or enemies. Each search really has the same object: survival.

"But," she continued, "*we* are never like the mountains. We come. We leave. The mountains are always brothers and sisters."

"You seem to understand me better than my husband does."

Tiana laughed lightly. "Don't be deceived. A good man understands things about you that a strange woman will never see. Keep missing him, Sarah. But never forget, he hunts for his own survival. *You* are a mountain and will always be a mountain."

We walked in silence to the base of the first mountain. "Come," she said, "let us go mountain climbing."

The slope was amazingly gentle, yet on arrival I looked down and realized I had never been higher. Tiana stared so intensely toward the southwest that I decided to give her space. Turning toward the southeast, I tried to affect the older woman's energy.

"See whatever it is you most want to see," a breeze-like voice enwrapped me. Was it Tiana's or Mother's? My heart answered, "Love and fortitude will make it clear."

I concentrated and there he was, my kidnapped brother Robin. Riding on a big roan with a smile on his face, he headed north, trailed behind our big green coach whose door bore a lion and a lamb. A tear fell. Before it struck earth, Tiana stood behind me and touched my neck. I felt a sensation akin to a wisp on a thread.

"It is time to return," she said.

The descent was even easier than the climb. Near the bottom we saw Sam Houston looking up at us. Out of his hearing, Tiana said, "If and when my husband goes to Texas it will be without me."

Voluntarily leaving a husband was something removed from my experience. I stopped and looked at her. "My own survival denies taking land from others. Such a person is as much a dream thief as one who kidnaps Africans and makes them slaves. Where are your ancestors now? Mine are here. That is why your mother spoke of Africa."

We arrived where the famous man stood. Houston had obviously been drinking. "There you are. I must take back my wife, Sallie."

"My name is Sarah."

"I'm sorry; I forgot. I once knew a Sallie. Please excuse my wife; she likes to talk."

"Says the hunter," said Tiana. He tried to kiss her, but she put her hands between them and said, "Your breath tells unwanted stories." He looked on child-like. "Others are starting to call you The Big Drunk; an honorable name like The Raven should not be thrown away."

I had been taught by my mother that a woman should never take face away from a man. Of course, the case could be made that he had done so to himself. Although I was embarrassed for him, I might just as well have been invisible. Perhaps he was so preoccupied with planning his next move that he overlooked the counsel of the woman who loved him and had taken in a heart-broken, once-powerful man who did not recognize that he had fallen from grace into grace.

"I don't care what the world thinks of me so long as they know I'm honest."

"Honesty does not settle all things," said Tiana. "Integrity includes more than what comes from the mouth."

He paused before saying, "Come with me, wife. I want you to hear this opening for a speech. He made a bow with his left arm and turned expecting her to place her right arm inside. "Never submit to an oppression—"

The sound of a ripping that bordered on a screech cut him off mid-sentence. Tiana said, "Here is something to take with you."

He looked back and found her extending one half of the thin blanket she had been carrying. Without a word, shoulders slumped, Houston headed off alone.

Confused I asked, "I missed something important." She was silent and I continued, "Shouldn't a wife follow her husband?"

"Once upon a time, he was my husband. Even before this day I had come to realize that when he is among the Cherokees, he calls me wife. Although I am a member of one of our nation's leading families, he leaves me behind while he goes to visit our arch-enemy, Andrew Jackson, where he asks for a 'loan' which some of my friends refer to as a bribe. On other occasions, he leaves me behind while he goes to Washington where he reports he is the Cherokee advocate, yet returns and those who are working hardest for our removal still call him friend. If I wove these images into a pattern on a blanket even a child could read them.

"The view from the mountaintop made the truth even clearer. I saw what he does not know: in Texas he will permit the slavery the Mexicans have outlawed, reduce the Comanches, and in the end fail to stand with the Cherokees. I saw from the mountain top that as a soldier he could storm the ramparts against an outnumbered foe but lacks the courage to bring me with him whenever white men sit in judgment. He will long for me, even send for me while secretly praying I will refuse to come. My people sheltered him. He will abandon us and blame us for the break. My love will be the unrecognized cost in all he wins and all he loses. I am his beauty, and he will become more of a 'Big Drunk'."

I looked back at the twin mountains. Even the one we had climbed had vanished in the midst of an advancing rain.

WHO ARE WE?

Patience Starbuck proposed she travel south posing as a slave mistress, accompanied by my brother Dan and me in search of my kidnapped brother Robin. I had thought she was insane. Could a Quaker and two fugitives with forged free papers yet masquerading as slaves, hope to do what seemed impossible? With advice from my father-in-law, she modified her vision and took on the Afro-Shawnee Caesar to drive her beautiful Lion and the Lamb coach. Caesar had led our escape from slavery. In my mind he could do anything. Despite a series of adventures, we had accomplished the task.

Nearly three decades after the fact, I marvel how, playing the coquette, Patience had accomplished purchasing Robin from a widowed master who had considered my brother his most valuable possession. Vainly the Georgia "cracker" had hoped to parley her offer of the market price into usurping her body. When William Shakespeare wrote, "What fools these mortals be," perhaps he was playing soothsayer and envisioning the reprobate who was hooked and released by our incomparable friend.

The rich Kentucky greenery reminded me of my wedding dress. That sparked thoughts of my husband and child. We were only a few days from crossing the Ohio River which itself was a single day from our home in Waynesville. My longing seemed to increase by the hour.

"This stretch is so serene that I should ask Caesar to slow the coach," said Patience.

She made the request and reluctantly Caesar obliged. For a few miles, we heard the wildlife above the horses' clomps It was a special time near the end of a journey that I imagined put that of Odysseus to shame. I knitted a new sweater for my child and enjoyed the day. My sylvan reverie was destroyed by unforgettable smells and sound: decaying flesh and hunting dogs. The coach was downwind of both, but not so far away that Caesar's conscience would allow him to keep to the northward course. In his youth, he had been one of Tecumseh's warrior on killing fields that marked the end of Indian control of the Eastern United States. He guessed that the dogs had been bred to hunt colored people, but he could not discern if the corpse was black, white, Shawnee, Creek, Cherokee or one of 100 different designations. He had been around scores of dead and knew from hard experience, dust to dust, they were all the same.

Caesar stopped the coach, gathered his weapons and went to Patience's window. "Ma'am, I'm gonna take the brothers and go off a ways. We'll be back soon."

The men went into a primeval forest on foot. They could hear the dogs barking just over the rise. In the clearing, a dead black man lay amidst grazing buzzards. The low grasses were disturbed as though he had tried to bury himself back first. Caesar clapped his hands and let out a Shawnee warrior's shout. The scavengers flew off.

Robin, my oldest brother, saw the body and exclaimed, "My Lord! He stuck a knife 'tween a chain link."

"Yep," said Caesar, "but he didn't die as soon as expected."

A thin knife had been jammed deep into the throat. Caesar bent down on one knee, extracted the knife and placed it next to the body. He had encountered other men who had taken their own lives. Most had been frightened white soldiers, afraid of being taken alive and the possibility of torture. Some had been white women afraid that if made the captive wife of a Shawnee, the hatred of her own people would so ruin her reputation that even escape would be ignoble. Here was a man seen as property who was unlikely either to be murdered or further stigmatized.

"His sense of honor was at stake," said Caesar.

"I hope he didn't leave anybody behind," said Dan.

"If he ran away alone, all of that was already decided," said Caesar.

The dogs came into view. They growled and showed their teeth. Behind them were their four scraggly-looking masters, thinking they were holding the hounds back. The dogs were certainly half-wild, but they were not crazy. The three colored men appeared fearless. This was a new attitude that chilled the dogs. Their leader was not as quick to correctly assess the situation. He said to his employees, "I knew two days' lead weren't enough!" Then he looked toward Caesar and said, "You niggers kill that nigger?"

"No," said Caesar coolly.

"Who the hell do you think you are?" said the slave catcher.

"Me? I'm just Caesar." He opened his stance and the slave hunters saw that he had both a red stained tomahawk and a hunting knife in his belt. Furthermore, in his right hand was a rifle poised at 60 degrees above the earth.

Long ago, Caesar had learned the power of speaking a single Shawnee word to a man who could not translate it. Menacingly he said, "*Pepkwaanwi.*" Of course, the rifle was capable of shooting, but it sounded like much more.

The slave catcher leader's voice dropped an octave as he said, "Okay men, cut off what's left of the brand. Let's hope it proves to his master we got the right coon."

"No," said Caesar.

All four slave catchers carried rifles and held onto leashed hound dogs. Dan's and Robin's only weapons were sheathed hunting knives. In a vacuum, four rifles against one rifle appeared good odds, but Caesar had a singularly untamed look in his eyes. Although he was dressed in his blue driver's pants and suspenders that made him seem best prepared to porter for a big city hotel, judging by his skin he was a black anomaly: a man with total disdain for white numbers. The two groups faced off with the slave catchers straining not to fidget and Caesar waiting to see how serious they were. Finally, the slave catcher leader said, "Hell fire! You expect us to walk away from a $50 reward?"

"No," said Caesar, "I expect y'all to walk away with your lives. My guess is that to you they're worth more than $50."

"We's got families to feed," protested the slave catcher.

Caesar reached into his pocket with his off-hand and extracted a roll of money. "Here's $20, that oughtta feed 'em." He tossed it underhanded toward the slave catcher and added, as the man missed the money and had to bow to retrieve it, "If you need more, shoot some possums and pick some poke salad." Pointing with his chin he continued, "Your families'll be better off than this poor soul y'all hounded to death."

"But—"

"I'm tired of talking," said Caesar. "Take your hounds and go." He brought his rifle up another 35 degrees and aimed it at the leader's heart.

Shaking, the leader said, "We're outta here, men."

Caesar turned to Robin. "My friend, go back to the coach for the shovel while we tidy up this man."

They buried the runaway. Dan asked, "Caesar, why weren't you afraid?"

"Were you?"

"I was simply busy acting like I believe my daddy would."

Caesar laughed. "Listen good, boys. I took the measure of each *wii'ishi*..."

"That's what you call a white man?" asked Robin.

"I'm sorry," said Caesar. "A *wi'ishi* is a dog. Those particular white men give dogs a bad name. I measured dogs and men. As long as those men held them dogs, they might as well been a piece of their arms. I doubt their guns was loaded while running through the woods. Then to shoot they woulda have to let loose the dogs, pull up the guns and aim. By then, I coulda killed one with the tomahawk, another with the knife, and shot a third. I'm supposing you boys wouldn't been just standing there watching."

"That's all?" said Robin.

"It ain't quite that simple," admitted Caesar. "Ain't nothing but a warrior can shoot good under pressure. Those four struck me as more bullies than warriors. I still had the suicide's knife. If the dogs had more heart than I give 'em credit for, I coulda handled them too."

"All the time I thought we were outnumbered," said Dan.

"But they didn't," said Caesar. "Did you think they was silent 'cause they was Quakers 'waiting on the Lord'? They knew I coulda killed at least one. They didn't wanna take a chance on me saying, 'Eenie, meenie, miney, you'."

They laughed. "You're a serious warrior, aren't you?" asked Dan.

"No," said Caesar, "I was a serious *na nah tah*. Now *nee lah e nee nee lah*."

"What does that mean?" asked Robin.

"It means, 'I am what I am', in all situations. More important, I wanna make sure y'all know that you showed courage in the face of danger. Now that you been tested you ain't got a reason to doubt yourself in the future. Your heart ain't a guess; it's a fact. It's a lucky man that don't face death but once in life. It didn't win this time, but soon it'll be back calling your name 'til you gives the only answer that'll satisfy it. Coward or warrior, death will be satisfied. Make the taking honorable."

◊◊◊◊◊◊

At the noonday break the next day, Caesar shared his reflections on the day before. "To protect a dead man's corpse, I was willing to kill four men and maybe sentence generations of their people to a life of suffering. Wars been fought for less, but I thought I was past killing folk in cold blood."

I did not believe it was my place to speak, but since the others were silent, I spoke my mind, "Why show empathy for everybody? Some people don't deserve kindness because they don't show it."

"The white man has driven us too far," he said to all of us. "That don't mean we're supposed to forget who we are. Never define yourself by the worst in somebody else."

My brothers were the sons of a long line of warriors. I judged by their faces that neither had considered the possibility that in a wilderness far from witnesses, a real man might have the opportunity to kill hated whites yet come to the conclusion that the better choice was negotiation.

I turned back to Caesar who spoke what sounded like a prayer, "Moneto, I need your help. These are violent times to practice peace, but where has killing got us?"

This time I joined the others in keeping quiet.

FREEDOM DAY

We had come a long way from Fruits of the Spirit Plantation. Not far enough, but the day was full of promise. I came down to Cincinnati from my chosen home in Waynesville to enjoy a celebration close in geography to where one of the worst incidents in my life had taken place.

My brother, Dan Crispin, was hosting on July 14, 1842 his fourth "Annual United States Freedom Day." Fifteen years earlier, Dan, our brother Robin and I had escaped Virginia slavery with Caesar, the Afro-Shawnee and his wife Monni, leading us to Ohio, the Promised Land. This did not make us extraordinary. I presume a few of Dan's guests, whether born to free or slave parents, had legitimate papers, but most of his friends and acquaintances, also had a forged free paper. Regardless of birth, American law required blacks to carry a passport and post $500 bond in the event we broke the law.

Through a loan from the white Quaker businesswoman, Patience Starbuck, Dan had risen to become one of the leading colored businessmen in Ohio. For the most part, whites ignored him or considered him an uppity nigger, living in imitation of what he could never be.

The entire colored community would hold a second celebration on August 1, commemorating the abolition of slavery in the British West Indies. The holiday celebrated at the Crispins' home was the day that imports of slaves were supposed to have ended in the United States. We celebrants did not need the Amistad Incident in 1839 to realize that the official ending of slave trade in 1808 was a sham. We all knew people who had been illegally imported. Indeed, many looked at the lack of white people's will for justice and expected slavery to still be thriving when our grandchildren's grandchildren became grandparents.

Dan's previous celebrations were far more intimate, but this year, as a show of unspoken defiance to those bully boys who hated to see colored people celebrate anything but national holidays and who he held responsible for our brother Robin's kidnapping and murder, Dan had convinced his wife Zephyrine to let him invite all of his employees and friends to the gathering. Joining in the moment, she had also extended invitations to her friends. Because the day fell on a Thursday, the Lion and the Lamb stage coach routes which were the source of family income were being run by men who sometimes substituted in emergencies.

The crowd did not begin to swell until most of the invitees had gotten off work. The vast majority of the men worked in slaughterhouses and on the docks. The females mostly were housemaids, wet nurses and laundry women. They all changed into their Sunday finest. Thankfully part of Cincinnati's charm was embedded in the lengthy summer daylight hours, and the fact that even people of color rarely worked a slave's schedule.

◊◊◊◊◊◊

The celebration's featured entrée had been prepared before dawn by Dan's favorite butcher and fellow Underground Railroad conductor, the German Jacob Rice. With his journeyman and two apprentices assisting, Rice had slaughtered a small drove of pigs. The quartered swine were placed in the boiling water of forty-gallon wash pots.

Once the hair was loose enough to scrape off, they were heaved out of the pot. This was one of the favorite times for the two young Crispin sons. Intently watching as the pigs were dumped on the ground, and pretending to be Shawnee warriors, they competed to be the first to "count coup" with a bare hand on a steaming hog. The winner won a dollar from the other. Some of the guests only earned that much in a half day of serious labor, but more were appreciative that some of us were successful than envious that children treated money so frivolously.

Crispin servants sliced and arranged on platters smoked hams from an earlier visit by Rice's crew. They carved some of the fresh pork into bacon, ribs and hams. All the bacon and a small portion of the ribs and hams were placed in the family's private smoke house. The ribs were barbecued Virginia style, extending them by a rope and slow roasting them over a hot fire.

I had helped prepare the already smoked hams, as well as various complimentary dishes but was fascinated to watch them all work. My mother had alternated between being head cook and field hand. As a child I felt I was above both responsibilities. As a slave, I had been given no choice. The work I was assigned from age eight was in the field.

Arriving guests sipped on various beverages and told stories about fantastic amounts of ribs "freed from captivity." The tales were alleged to have originated on various famous plantations whose owners were claimed to be richer than John Jacob Astor or crueler than any Russian Czar. I was happy to be around other colored people when most of my life in Waynesville, Ohio was among whites. Lies fascinated me as much as truth.

Although Zephyrine wanted Dan to keep company with church members, my brother was angry with God both for not freeing black slaves as He was alleged to have done for Jewish slaves and for ignoring his prayers when he and Robin were gunned down on the streets of Cincinnati. He had survived a horrible wound but Robin, for whom we had risked everything to rescue, had not.

To his wife's consternation, several of Dan's drinking buddies from Gates' Saloon had been invited to the celebration and had staked claim to a corner of their huge yard.

Dan excused himself from his seat in the center of the festivities surrounded by fellow members of the Iron Chest Society of colored men devoted to Underground Railroad activities. He went to make certain his friends from Gates' were comfortable. Knowing from Zephyrine that these men were among the city's least successful and most colorful, without invitation, I joined my brother. From afar we heard their banter.

"Throwin' down ribs is how Eat-'em-Up got his name," said Toad making up the story on the spot.

"Could that also be how he lost his toofeses?" said Sweetnin' Water.

"Nah," said Toad. "He had a tooth ache and went to a blind dentist who kept pullin' 'til he got the right one!"

We laughed along with them. That a man of Dan's class was friendly enough to both spend many an evening beside common laborers and invite them to a wonderful celebration insured their best behavior. My being a woman served to reinforce it.

"Sweet Sarah!" said Eat-'em-Up leading the others in standing to acknowledge my presence.

"You may sit, sirs," I said.

"You men have all you need?" Dan looked at each.

"Now that we got somethin' pretty to look at we's fine," said Toad complimenting me with his eyes.

"It appears Eat-'em-Up failed to tell you this is my sister, *Mrs.* Sarah Ferguson," said Dan.

"No offense, Dan." Toad held up his hands as though Dan were the sheriff.

"As for everythin' we need," said Eat-'em-Up, "how could we, when you got all the money and Zee to boot!"

Everyone laughed. Dan turned, looked admiringly at his wife standing twenty yards away and then back at his friends. "I'd call for a new game," he said, "but we all know who'd win that one too."

They laughed heartily and he added, "Just let me know if you're still hungry or thirsty. I'll see to it you are satisfied."

"Dan," said Toad smiling. "Miss Zee done closed off all alcohol so you know our thirst can't be touched no more than a colored man can get in the White House."

"Two things I can't do," said Dan, "is quench the thirst of a man who could drown in whiskey and take a seat in the White House when I can't even vote for myself."

He turned away amidst their laughter.

"I'd like to sit a spell with these good men," I said to my brother. He shrugged and continued on.

"You ain't no spy is you?" said Eat-em-Up.

"My mother did not permit tattling," I said, making myself comfortable.

"Good," said Sweetnin' Water. "Course, we ain't never done nothin' yo' mama would disapprove."

I joined them in laughter.

"I told you he wouldn't overrule Zee," said Eat-'em-Up.

"If she was mine I'd tell her what to do," said Toad.

"If that sweet thang was your'n, the rooster would crow at dawn," said Eat-'em-Up, "and tell you one more dream done ended."

◊◊◊◊◊◊

An hour later, the Gates Saloon crew sat at a table as they enjoyed a plate of ribs, collard greens, and cornbread so perfect Eat-'em-Up claimed, "Zee musta done spit in it."

Ignoring a fine cloth napkin, Sweetnin' Water wiped his mouth with the back of his shirt sleeve and said, "Man, I ain't had this good a time since we had to dig my master's fat wife out the bottom of the outhouse."

"What was she doin' there?" said Eat-'em-Up.

"Tryin' to show poop don't stank worse than her turnip-green eatin' ass," said Sweetnin' Water.

When the group stopped laughing, Gates said, "I'd ask why I ain't heard that story before, but I already know the answer."

"I wonder why Lillith ain't here," mused Toad.

"I see why you ain't never been married. You ain't got the sense God gave a giant that drowns in a thimble," said Eat-'em-Up.

"Cause she pretty and what she do for a livin'?" said Toad.

"A married man better not even act like he wanna throw a party and invite another woman, ugly as a starvin' bug or fine as wine, Christian as Jesus's mama or otherwise," said Sweetnin' Water.

"He's telling the Lord's truth," said Gates. "I bet your best pair of overalls that every woman walking around here got Queen Zee's seal of approval,"

The men turned and looked admiringly across the yard at Zephyrine. She was less than fifty yards away, dressed like a model in Godey's and laughing while discussing something with Patience Starbuck. Gates turned back to "Eat-'em-Up and said, "I've been meanin' to ask, what was that dance you were doin' a li'l while ago?"

"Look like the rigor mortis to me," said Toad.

"If it was, yo' mama forgot to name it," said Eat-'em-Up. "She the one done taught me when she got tired of layin' on her back."

Before Toad could reply, Gates said, "All right, men, we're guests, and this ain't my saloon and you promised Sarah you would be good." I simply smiled and they continued to ignore my presence,

"Kentucky is the land of dancers" said Eat-'em-Up. "I can dance rings 'round everybody here."

"Ring-'round-the-Rosie,' is a girly dance," said Sweetnin' Water.

"Y'all always messin' with me," said Eat-'em-Up.

"Let him alone," said Gates. Eat-'em-Up's eyes expressed a hint of gratitude until Gates said, "The only reason those Kentucky boys dance so good is it's against state law for white or black to wear shoes outside."

"Yeah," said Toad, "they always is hoppin' round dodgin' pieces of briar patches and snakes."

Eat-'em-Up laughed with the others and then, twisting Gates' insinuation said, "It is true that clothes don't make the man. Broganed or barefoot, a Kentucky man is all man."

"Speaking of shoes," said Gates, "Look at Dan over there. He's wearing those special shoes. His brother made me some just like that."

"Dan got a brother?" said Toad.

"He got more than one, but the only one I ever met got gunned down. I knowed him."

"Them bully boys and slave catchers was cold as snow on Mama's grave," said Eat-'em-Up.

My heart pounded. Hoping to get them to change to any other subject under the sun, I said quietly, "I was there."

The men entered a respectful silence before Sweetnin' Water said, "If you had shoes like that, Gates, how come I ain't never seen 'em?"

"I'm glad you asked that question. Some fool stole 'em, and you was a suspect til just now."

"Damn," said Sweetnin' Water, "a suspect in the white man's eyes and a suspect in the colored man's eyes too? How they done stole millions of us from Africa and the whole country from the Injins and Sweetnin' Water is a suspect? Five'll get you ten the sheriff is wearin' them shoes when he goes to church."

The laughter was not as raucous as it had been. Still the subject of shoes made by my murdered brother was too close for my comfort. Gates looked at me. "Them boots gets set off good with them fine duds you made for him and Zee."

"Thank you." I seized the moment to leave them. "If you men will excuse me, I had better join the others,"

They stood for my departure. Gates said, "Ma'am, I hope my bringing up your brother's death didn't bother you."

I did not want to lie so I said nothing. My eyes were dry when I left them. Still I wondered if one day I might find a resolution for Robin's murder. Knowing it would have to include forgiveness of those who had stolen so much of our family's joy, I disappointed myself by allowing a tear to fall.

SPRING

Fannie, my older sister, escaped slavery separately from my three brothers and me. For a time, she established herself in Cincinnati but fled west when her husband turned abusive. Accompanying her was Val, who had once been my best friend and the latter's daughter Sally. The baby's father was my brother, Dan Crispin. He had seduced Val prior to marrying Zephyrine and never met the child.

In St. Louis, Fannie and Val had fallen in love with two colored mountain men. My sister told me this story that was so far removed from my experiences that I had to ask her to read it and verify what I had heard.

They were two families led by twin brothers who had fled Mississippi slavery, my sister, a runaway slave from Kentucky, and a woman who had discovered that in Ohio her bondage was illegal. The men were trappers in the Rocky Mountains and the women frontier homemakers. In 1846, the Lucky families moved to a new makeshift camp on a tributary that had plenty of sweet bark cottonwood for the horses to eat. The night before the brothers left to set the year's first traps, Fannie lay in Marshall's arms. "I do love these mountains."

"Watchou love best 'bout t'em?" said Marshall.

"Your loving feeling. I never want to lose it."

The men planned to stay out for five days at a time, trapping along the river and coming home for two days with their families. During the third set of seven, Fannie and Val went to the local creek to wash. They used soap made from buffalo and bear fat, plant oils, ashes, and for scent, the season's first bitter root wild flowers. Old habits die hard. As she wrung the last drip out of clothing, Fannie internally fought to prevent herself from pretending the clothes were the necks of her first slave holder, Nathan Prescott, the man who had repeatedly raped our mother and in his will sold our family apart. When she told me about her fantasy I told her not only did I share it but I also imagined sewing up his private parts, front and rear and watching him explode. In time, I had grown ashamed of my day dreams. Now my overarching feeling is, "Heaven help us all."

By the time Fannie spread clothing on bushes or saplings, somehow her gentle nature returned. Observers might have concluded she washed dainty cloths.

"This cold frosty mountain water makes me feel my innards," said Val.

"At least we know only we own them," said Fannie.

"I keep thinking 'bout that li'l bitty bar of soap that Patience Starbuck sent us. I'm glad you told me it wasn't for washin' clothes. She did some wild things when I lived on Caesar's Creek. For a bit she had me scared she done gone sure 'nough crazy."

"Say what you will, but that soap made the men feel good."

◊◊◊◊◊◊

That night a set of three rapidly delivered screams awakened the women and children. Initially Fannie thought it was one of her nightmares. Yet another high-pitched screech pierced the air.

"I'd rather listen to wolves and wolverines than whatever that powerful scary creature is," said Val. There it was again. "It sounds like somebody in mortal misery."

"I wish the men were here," said Fannie. A single scream split the air. "They ain't here, but we are. Get your gun, Val, and I'll get mine."

The women grabbed their rifles and Val's daughter Sally picked up her bow and arrows. In the dark, the creature came closer. Fannie lit a candle. Again, they heard a tortured scream. The two toddlers started to cry, and Val said, "Buck up, boys. Y'all ain't motherless chillen! Ain't nothin' touchin' y'all 'lessen it come through us."

The horses kicked up their heels and whinnied. The screams disappeared. Against everyone's counsel, my sister Fannie took the candle outside. Less than twenty yards from the cabin, she found mountain lion tracks under the tree and claw marks on the bark leading to where Val had placed most of a deer she had killed the previous day.

"It's a good thing I brought that haunch in," said Val. "I got plans for what that scoundrel didn't get."

◊◊◊◊◊◊

At daybreak, Val said to Fannie, "I'm going sneak up on the twins. What a surprise I'm gonna spring."

Fannie said, "Shouldn't we both go?"

"You went alone the last time."

"But I invited you to come along with me."

"The onliest reason I didn't was 'cause I didn't want to leave Sally alone watchin' the li'l ones, or worse yet, bring a whole colored circus to a work place."

"Children are our peace," said Fannie.

"True that, but if you don't mind, watch the chillen," said Val. "I got my mind stayed on walkin' by myself anyway. After we feed 'em, I'm gonna use some of our special soap, put on my Bannock dress I bought at the '36 Rendezvous, and carry that haunch in a baby backpack. The twins gotta be tired of they own sorry cookin', and I know Sip'll be happy for a li'l surprise away from pryin' eyes."

Both smiled, and it was settled. When breakfast ended, Val began the five-mile journey. It was a clear day with fading patches of snow vainly attempting to hide in the shadows. Fannie knew that our mother trusted intuition. Perhaps being born in America caused her to be less sure of her own intuition. She prevented herself from speaking the three short words on her mind, "Don't go, Val."

◊◊◊◊◊◊

In relating what had occurred that day, Fannie imagined Scipio and Marshall as they launched into "Wade in the Water" and then sang their entire repertoire, including their work in progress, "No Salt in the Beans". Many nights the brothers had regaled their wives with these songs. Fannie and Val believed they would carry the lyrics to their graves. The lyrics always made them think of the six siblings and the mother they doubted they would again see. They never tired of trying to build on the lyrics.

"No salt in the beans,
but the water is low.
No salt in the beans,
but they helping me grow.

"Jump back, Marshall,
Sip, don't be late.
These beans ain't long
for this here plate.

"If it wasn't for these beans
Mama mighta died.
If it wasn't for these beans,
Daddy woulda cried."

The twins, now fathers themselves, had never asked the identity of their own sire. Was he the breeder who lived across the county, or the man their mother loved who had been sold for disobedience? Did their mother know? Did it matter? Whoever he was, he was as invisible as the God to which all the slaves and our relatives spent every conscious moment praying. Their mother was their only parent and by all accounts she had done a fine job.

On the fateful day, the twins had been at work from last darkness when they had eaten jerked beaver and chased it with three cups of coffee. They were warmly dressed in their bearskin overcoats and leggings with beaver skin hats sheltering their heads from the cold air. Their wives had made some of their clothing but they were experienced mountain men, fully capable of performing work that men back in the settlements would have considered beneath them. In recounting their daily activities, they had told their wives they always removed their gloves as they walked in water so icy that each time they stepped out, the chill stung their hairy legs beneath the leggings.

"We do this for y'all," Val's husband had once said.

"Then who was you doing it for before y'all knew us?"

They checked the five pound traps which they had scented with musk designed to signal a four-legged intruder and placed near the shore at dusk the previous night. Before each visit to a trap, they prayed that the inquisitive animals had drowned quickly after being snared. Any sign of struggle, such as a gnawed off paw, caused momentary sadness. Years among the Indians had given them sensitivity to the life sustaining animals. Killed animals were thanked for giving up their lives that people might live.

Trapping was ending in the Rockies but the twins had as a goal to harvest thirty packs or 1500 beaver this season. Their wives doubted the possibility of such bounty. In harmony with their mothers' example, Fannie and Val kept their questioning to themselves and cheered them on.

◊◊◊◊◊◊

Fannie learned what happened next from a Bannock warrior named Swift Eagle. In sight of Scipio and Marshall's labors, Val witnessed it all. A dozen Bannocks broke through the cottonwoods. She snatched the back pack off, removed the rifle rope, aimed, fired, and reloaded. Simultaneously and before the colored trappers knew what was happening, a withering flurry of arrows and bullets riddled their bodies.

Another woman might have tried fleeing or hiding, but Val was armed and determined.

She fired her second shot. Not knowing the strength of the opposition, most of the Bannocks bolted. Their leader, Gray-Eyed Cougar, looked over his shoulder and saw one lone woman. He dropped his rifle and rode toward her with only his spear. Val coolly aimed at the oncoming horse and rider. Before she could fire her third shot, he ducked beneath his horse's neck. He need not have bothered. Her bullet would have missed him. It struck the horse between the eyes, sending the rider flying and crashing in a bruised heap. Limping, Gray-Eyed Cougar continued toward her on foot. Meanwhile Val grabbed her butcher knife from the food sack. He came within reach. She lunged and, in one movement, he dodged, grabbing her by the throat. With the other hand, he knocked the butcher knife out of her hand. He was about to choke her to death when a young warrior named Swift Eagle called out, "She is one of the colored women who saved many lives at the Horse Creek massacre!"

Gray-Eyed Cougar hesitated. Remembering the dead and how the black men had helped kill his friends and relatives, he succumbed to blood lust. Before Swift Eagle could stop him, he strangled Val.

"There is no honor in this killing," said Swift Eagle.

"My honor is in her dead men, and the bigger one's scalp belongs to me."

"Are you sure you have killed the right men?"

"The only wrong in this killing was the third man was away, and it was he who took my best friend's scalp."

Both male scalps were lifted and their bodies sliced as though a butcher had gone berserk. Val was left where she lay, desecrated only by the theft of her life.

I remember the night Fannie had told me this story. Before this I had mistakenly believed that only whites could be cruel.

◊◊◊◊◊◊

Back at the cabin, morning passed slowly. The day's rhythm remained in perpetual cleaning and mending; cooking and feeding; encouraging and disciplining; moving through the stages of making fur robes; teaching, planning, and initiating.

The second meal ended. Fannie put the little ones down for a nap and left Sally to babysit. She walked to the creek, carrying a bucket of water on her head as she thought, 'What a beautiful day to be alive and free.' A bird call reminded her of the toy trumpet that her second master's son had played. She mused over children starting out kind and growing up to be someone who was thrilled by oppressing. 'Somewhere in the teaching is hate and not love. Somewhere Nyame is pushed aside and Anansi allowed free reign.' Not far off the trail, she spied the feathered musician. 'Look at that black bird with white feathers on her back and a few red in his crown,' she thought awestruck at the site of the downy woodpecker. 'If Nyame can let one creature embrace all that glory, why can't folk everywhere get along like we do out here in these mountains?' She answered her own question. 'Anansi, why can't you grow up? Making us hurt each other shouldn't make you laugh.'

I marveled that my sister still thought of Nyame and Anansi, the Fante deities that I had abandoned in my youth. What good were they here in a land that always treats us as foreigners?

She returned and found the boys still asleep and Sally busy at her chore. "No Val?"

"No Mama."

"Your mother should have returned by now." The six-year-old child silently looked at her aunt and continued her work, scraping clean the skin of a bighorn sheep. Fannie turned to check on the three-year-old boys. Suddenly her son woke up. Without apparent reason, he hit his sleeping cousin. Fannie cried.

'What's wrong with me?' she asked herself before restoring peace. Following the apology and a hug, Fannie said to Sally, "Something is not right." The child saw her aunt's still wet eyes. She hesitated before following her practice when unhealed trauma made Fannie cry in her sleep and the other adults were absent. She started to come over to comfort her, but Fannie held up her hand, and Sally stopped.

"Stay with the boys and," said Fannie. "And you, Kofi and William, if you gentlemen don't treat each other gentle, there are ways to make you wish you had."

"Yes, ma'am," they said in unison.

"Sally, I'm riding to check on the others."

Fannie saddled her horse and left for the river.

The lack of sound in the forest was unsettling. To Fannie this quiet was at least as old as Cain and Abel. 'Where are the birds?' she thought. 'Has the whole world, except for what Val calls "Earth Angels," closed down?' A quickening breeze swirled the catkins until they threatened to blind her. Fannie slowed her horse from trot to walk. There, almost in response to her recent query was a bird's, "Bob-o-lee, bob-o-link. Bob-o-lee, bob-o-link."

"What a soothing song." She looked toward the bird. "But they don't stay long enough in the mountains."

Fannie came into the clearing. In horror, she dropped her rifle. Beyond quiet there is silence, the step before the deafness that presented itself when Fannie saw Val. Her friend's body lay akimbo in a patch of snow being mangled by wolves that had stripped her clothes and most of her flesh. The pieces of the dead screamed in one voice. That voice was Fannie's, "Agggghhh!" A false dusk swept in as traveling west, the sun dipped behind the most southwesterly peak.

"Oh, Val," said Fannie feinting at the wolves to scare them several yards away. She dismounted and began an attempt to tidy up the body. "If I had known this land would bring us to this spring day, I would never have suggested we leave St. Louis."

Without thinking, Fannie brushed frantically at the nearest bloody tracks of the wolves. Already on her knees she fell forward onto the stained grass. She released a sob and straightened her upper torso. Gazing around the meadow, blood seemed to be all over creation especially upon the wild snowberry and anemone flowers whose scent now seemed toxic. A passing cloud released a few rain drops. Weeping, she forced herself to stand and remembered that both wolves and vultures were also nearby. Through the sprinkle she released another scream. This one failed to wake up the dead but chased away the predators.

Along with Val's remnants, the flaked flesh of the men was guaranteed to become a part of her life's nightmares, mixing with tortured memories of her own sexual assaults, those of our mother and older sisters, the selling apart of our family, an abusive first marriage, and just being black in a land that despised us for it.

Fannie moved across the killing field, trembling incessantly and gathering up pieces of flesh here and bone there, not knowing what to do with them. It occurred to her to carry the men's pieces over to where Val's ravaged corpse lie. The sun cleared the first peak and sent a few rays through the clouds. Something metallic sparkled. Fannie redirected her steps. There was the wedding ring she had given Marshall. It was still attached to his divided left hand. She reached down to remove it from one of the two bloody fingers and felt faint. By the time her head stopped spinning again, she was on her knees weeping.

Momentarily reverting to her first tongue she said aloud, "Half the story cain't never be told. Still Marshall, honey, what happened, or do I really wanna know?"

She reached for the little good luck pouch that he wore around his neck. She dumped its contents: an old charm, locks of hair from the twins' mother, one of Marshall's curls, a few strands from their son, some of her own kinks, and an unknown key. She placed his good luck charms in her own pouch and removed the wedding ring that she had given him one sunny day in St. Louis. Placing it in his now empty pouch, she said, "I'll bury this with you. Take it wherever you may travel."

Fannie lacked a shovel and wondered what good a grave might do when the predators knew what had happened. She thought that cremation might be best. Before she could act, she looked up and saw a young Indian without war paint sitting on his horse. He silently watched her. Startled, she almost attempted to run away, but as taught by Marshall, she stopped, sat down on the ground and lowered her head, inviting the warrior to strike. His horse did not move. Time passed chaste and unnoticed. Finally she stood and said in Crow, the *lingua franca* of the region, "Friend, would you help me?"

He was not certain that he acted acceptably. He only knew that once, before he had proven himself a warrior, trappers had attacked his village, killed many, and this woman had come to his rescue. He dismounted and went into the woods to gather material to build a scaffold. While he brought several armloads of branches, Fannie sat dazed. Near the end, she joined in the careful construction of a resting place worthy of the name.

With the structure in place, he climbed back on his horse and watched Fannie course the killing field, gathering and tenderly placing the remains of her loved ones on the scaffold. She stood covered in blood, as he placed his own blanket on the remains of the dead. Finally he broke his silence by speaking in Crow, "May I return you to your children?"

Her head went dizzy again. In the shadows of the fallen, she had almost forgotten the living. Fannie inhaled and studied the tall, slender man. She had trusted him this far. She gave him the hand signal, "Not yet." Bowing her head, she sang in Fante a song our mother had taught her:

"We are not at home
and may never see
our river again,
but nothing will ever
separate our love
from the cooling waters.

"Remember me today
as you did before,
the one who chose to be

your good friend for life,
the one who chose to be
united in absence."

She finished and walked to the bier, whispering in Fante as though Marshall could hear, "Fare thee well a while, my Mississippi trapper. Love recalls what death denies."

She went back to the Bannock who waited with her horse. He motioned with his head for her to mount. "All die, but what I regret most is that they did not have time to sing their death songs."

With her voice clipped by the rising wind, Fannie said, "The three of them only sang about life."

From the change in his eyes' coloration, Fannie believed he was thinking, 'Did I hear her correctly?' Instead of repeating her words she thought, 'If I had my way either both Val and I would be dead or both alive. Now I only have the children to live for. Anansi, you win again.'

◊◊◊◊◊◊

"Friend," said Fannie, as they came into the clearing across from their camp, "I don't know what to do."

The Bannock, whose name was Swift Eagle, had already concluded that he had broken so many customs by helping her that he might as well do what he believed she would do for him under similar circumstances.

"I have watched you secretly for years. If I had not made it a habit, Gray-Eyed Cougar might not have known to come here. Now I owe you safety. Medicine Calf, the black white man who lives with the Crows will protect you. I will take you to the Crow village where he lives."

'Jim Beckwourth,' she thought. 'Anansi, you used spring to steal my love, my best friend, and her husband, and now you send me to a lecherous man I don't like? Every day will be winter. What did I ever do to hurt you?'

From the doorway, Sally saw Swift Eagle. She sat down on the ground and lowered her head in submission. "Stand," he said.

Deliberately he took his vermilion from his pouch and painted first Fannie's and then Sally's cheeks. 'With this man,' thought Fannie, 'I may be a slave but there will be peace.'

Swift Eagle watched Fannie's family prepare to leave. In harmony with Bannock children, even the three-year-old boys had their own small and gentle ponies. The boys were braced on saddles covered with one blanket, while a second blanket rested on their mounts' withers. Silently each sat erect and rode without human assistance. They were still within sight of their cabin when Fannie thought, 'This was my Garden of Eden. 'But even if it was Sodom, I deserve my memories.' She turned and let her eyes embrace all of the beauty of her life in this home that ended with the events of a single spring day.

Swift Eagle questioned the wisdom of his plan to take them to Beckwourth. All of his life he had hated the Crows and judged Medicine Calf as unreliable. Now he, a member of the *Panákwate*, was about to give Fannie to them. From surveillance, he knew every inch of Fannie's body. He also knew that despite the hours he had spent in observation, there were untold yards of her inner being that were uncharted. Yes, she was older, but not nearly old enough to be his mother. Frequently Swift Eagle would tell this story while the family was gathered around the fire. "I thought, 'This is a black-white woman with three children. Can I cross this invisible line into another spirit world? Can I place her story next to mine?'"

Swift Eagle brought his horse to a complete stop. He turned his head and looked back at Fannie. The last time he had studied her face she had seemed on the verge of defeat. Now he thought he saw hope. He turned his horse toward his own village. Despite the sound of the trailing horses, he could have sworn he heard Fannie sigh in relief.

'Nyame,' thought Fannie, 'praise your holy name. Like the sun clearing a peak, I have not set. It is truly spring. For that, I am grateful.'

POSSIBILITIES

In the summer of 1846, Caesar, the fourth in a line of African rooted Shawnees, and his Monacan wife, Monni, arrived unexpectedly in Waynesville, Ohio. More than a decade earlier, Caesar had led Patience Starbuck, my brother Dan Crispin and me through the south in an attempt to rescue our kidnapped brother, Robin. This noble venture had knit her into the fabric of "The House of Esi", our mother.

While we women cleaned up the dinner dishes, my husband Charles, said to Caesar, "Why doth thee continue going west? With all the Indian removals, is it not growing too dangerous for thee and Monni to move around south of the river?"

"Where is it safe for a colored man to move? As for south of the Ohio River, nothing there has ever frightened me. And we go west because the reservations are there. If I could keep my feet away from them I would. There is no deeper sadness than what you see in the faces of those removed from their homeland."

I loved Caesar as the father of my adulthood, but upon hearing his words I silently disagreed. My own sadness as child of a family of slaves sold apart with no ability to find let alone visit my lost relatives must be sadder. Later I felt ashamed of myself. How can one compare losses? Both of us lived in worlds where our possibilities had been kidnapped.

"I cannot stay away. From the land now called Canada to that which is called Florida and I fought beside the men confined on reservations. Together we buried some of the greatest warriors to ever draw breath. We chose different paths, but they will always be my brothers."

"Often, we move in the shadows," said Monni, "but at least we move."

◇◇◇◇◇◇

Knowing that my brother Dan would be happy to hear that his old friends were visiting, I sent a letter by his Lion and the Lamb Stage Coach which ran through Waynesville. Dan, had risen from teenage runaway to wealthy black businessman. As a conductor on the Underground Railroad he proved he had not forgotten his roots. He left his second in charge and brought his family north for the weekend. Patience Starbuck joined us for dinner.

When evening fell, I said, "It's time for the children to go to bed."

I waited patiently, but when my oldest daughter Susan failed to join the younger children, after a few minutes I said, "Did thee not hear me?"

"Mama," said Susan, "I'm 14. My teacher says that's old enough to be a woman in some societies. Why can't I stay up a little while longer?"

"This one time, but only for an extra hour," I said. "The chickens will need to be fed and the cow milked at the same time as always." I was not pleased with Susan's smile. "Remember, daughter, teachers rule schools; mothers rule homes."

"Yes, ma'am."

The room settled. Patience said, "I have been saving a package to show all gathered." She took out copies of prints that one of her New York lawyers had sent. Most were of decorated soldiers. Another was of her attorney with his family. The final print was of a slump-shouldered slave chained on an auction block. For everyone's inspection, she placed them on the kitchen table.

"Without commentary, my attorney sent this outrageous picture, as if to remind me we must be steadfast in our commitment to freeing the oppressed. I have spent all of my adult years struggling against slavery, first in Nantucket, then in Philadelphia, later here in Ohio and traveling as far as that hell-land of Georgia."

"It brings back horrid memories," I said.

"I hesitated to show it," said Patience.

"You need not have worried," said Dan. "Each day we draw breath something like it is on the mind of every colored person in America."

Caesar silently examined each print separately. "What say thee?" said Patience to him.

He studied them for several additional seconds before answering, "Knowing your feelings about war, I'm surprised you didn't burn these three photos with soldiers. Unless I'm mistaken, they fought against the Mexicans."

"Yes," said Patience. "They were a part of Polk's legions to extend the slaveocracy. If the President is successful in appropriating more land from the Mexicans, I predict the new territories will lead to war between the southlands and the north. I intend to use these pictures when I speak against the war next week in Dayton."

"Thee intends to mix slavery and war?" said Charles.

"If the power of mixing were mine," said Patience, "I would mix justice with love. Slavery is always lack of peace, which is to say, it *is* war."

"Since the Europeans arrived, there has never been peace in this land," said Caesar. There was a brief silence before he said, "The first time we were in the southwest, it was to visit Shawnees who were forced to live in northern Mexico. We crossed over into the land the Mexicans had themselves stolen from the tribes. Vincente Guerrero, their colored President, freed the slaves while we were there. He was so well loved that they named a state in his honor."

"I knew they change Presidents almost as often as Cincinnati changes weather, but they had a colored President?" said Dan shocked at the possibility.

"Yes, for a time," said Monni, "and two colored governors of California, including one who administers as we speak."

Dan said, "I wish I could say the sun shines on everyone—but it does not."

"I have faith that one day this country will have a colored governor—even a colored President," said Patience. Among all of those in the room, only my husband could vote. Her statement seemed so outrageous that it was unworthy of comment.

I said, "Did you meet Guerrero?"

"I have never met any President," said Caesar. "And I would not care to meet one. We were fooled when the white man came to Shawnee land and first spoke of Presidents as, 'The Great Father.' As a father, we looked for a man who loved us and protected us from harm. So we waited to meet our 'Father'. We never saw this man. What kind of father was this? The whites we see are always willing to kill us or steal our land. 'The Great Father' never personally led a war party. 'Aha!' said my mother, 'he must be a Peace Chief.'"

"I loved my mother-in-law," said Monni, "but she was mistaken."

"I have met Peace Chiefs from many bands and tribes," said Caesar, "Shawnee, Lenape, Creek, Wyandot, Potawatomie, Cherokee…always the Peace Chief must be mindful of the good of *all* people and speak straight truth. This is not so for Presidents. A lying, thieving Peace Chief would lose his office. Every President I've heard of sells sincerity but weaves words with deliberate lies."

"Was Vincente Guerrero this way too?" said Patience.

"I have interpreted for many treaties and in hundreds of meetings with different parties, but none had to do with him. What I can tell you is that not only did he free the slaves but he also built schools that taught *all* people, and he set up free libraries."

"If he hadn't been murdered he might have done more," said Monni, who had been adopted by Quakers after her family had been massacred. "I once saw the Mexican Constitution. It is much more just than the one in Washington. But the Texans disrespected the Mexican Constitution and said they would fight before they would free the slaves."

"I read that the Texans were invited into Mexico," said Dan.

"I think the Mexicans wanted the Texans on their frontier because they feared the Comanche Nation more than the whites," said Caesar. "If I had met Guerrero I would have told him, never underestimate white Americans. They are a shiftless people. Comanches may kidnap and take scalps. White Americans take everything."

Dan's wife, Zephyrine said, "Can I go back to what you said about Peace Chiefs and Presidents?"

"The night is young," said Caesar. He turned to smile at Susan and added, "for some."

"Uncle Caesar," said Susan. "You must be on Mama's side."

"Any man who does not side with mothers would be a poor warrior."

The room's laughter was interrupted by Zephyrine, "Amen to that truth. Why do you think there's such a difference between a President and a Peace Chief?"

"True warrior societies ignore the wants of the mothers, and both the United States and Mexico are warrior societies."

I said, "Don't most of the tribes have many war chiefs?"

"It is our way," said Caesar, "to honor men who have proven in war that they can lead a party of like-minded men to fight. It is the whites who call them 'war chiefs'. These men should not be compared to *the* Peace Chief, just as all officers in the United States or Mexican Military should not be compared to the President. Is a sergeant a chief?"

"So the Peace Chief is more like the tribe's President?" said Zephyrine.

"The Peace Chief is the *protector*," said Caesar. "No chief orders any warrior."

Patience said to Caesar, "I so wanted this to be a night dominated by peaceful conversation. Doth thee have any opinion of the other prints?"

"A man always has opinions," said Caesar. "Not all are worth speaking aloud."

"A word, please," said Patience.

"Some of my people believe photos can steal spirits. I do not. If I let someone take my photo I would be *surrendering* my spirit. I do not want my photograph taken because I am not a brick house like the one Patience lives in. I am a man. Men were made to move. I believe I would even lose much of my spirit on a reservation or a slave plantation. I will never sit for a photograph because I have no desire to add to being misunderstood."

"Bravo," said Patience. "Did thee know I have never had my photo taken? But it is vanity that prevents me. Why inflict my image on innocent eyes?"

The adults turned to look at Susan who said, "I will send myself to bed now, before being misunderstood becomes my burden."

The gathering laughed and watched her leave the room.

"Now that the child has left, we need a plan," I said. "What do you think is the best strategy to free the slaves?"

I realized even before I spoke that the question itself seemed outrageous. Throughout the country even some slaveholders questioned their own behavior. Of course, all of them wanted to be paid for their losses and none of them considered the possibility of paying the slaves for theirs.

Patience said, "I would start with making those who are already free, equal."

"Here! Here!" said Dan.

"To accomplish this we need God on our side."

"No," said Caesar. People turned in astonishment. "We need to find the side of the one you call God and stand *with* the Great Spirit. Then all things will be possible."

There was a lengthy silence that Dan broke. "Talk of freeing the slaves costs less than breathing air. Look around this room; what do you see?"

"You tell us, husband," said Zephyrine. "What do you see?"

He paused before giving his answer. "A black housewife, a displaced Shawnee, an even more displaced Monican, a black seamstress, her white Quaker husband, a middle aged white Quaker businesswoman, and me. What can such a motley group do? Each of us stands outside the circle of power; only one of us can vote and even his voice is barely respected, being a Quaker who refuses to pick up a weapon."

"Interesting," said Patience. "Thee sees a mountain with no top. I see possibilities…endless possibilities. For we are united in a love for justice and, with The Lord's help, we will resist anyone and anything that is opposed to it. As Caesar suggested, should we unite with God's side we cannot lose. That One has never been a loser. Am I fooling myself and standing alone?"

She looked around the room. I saw in each person's eyes love for her vision, love for her commitment, love for her being. I took my husband's hand, kissed it and said, "I am a woman of possibilities."

FREEDOM SEEDS

In November of 1847, Carrie knocked on the rear door of the brick house with the commanding view. Mandy, Patience Starbuck's cook, answered. To her surprise a colored woman with no sign of being harried stood before her.

"You've come to a special place. How may I help you, ma'am?" said Mandy.

"That stagecoach man said Miss Patience Starbuck owns this here house and she be somebody who helps runaways."

Patience arrived in time to hear the last words.

"Come in dear," said Patience. "Rain is threatening."

"No it ain't," said Carrie. "It's been raining all my life but it ain't goin' to rain no more."

Patience stepped back and Carrie stepped into the biggest pantry she had ever seen. She stared wide eyed at the provisions. Patience said, "Is thee hungry?" Before the visitor could answer Patience said to Mandy, "Supper is nearly prepared is it not?"

"Yes, ma'am," said Mandy. "Please set the table for another."

Carrie's said, "I know you ain't plannin' for me to eat with you?"

"And why not?"

"I'm just a nigger. Everybody knows we don't be eatin' with no white folks."

"Please, dear…your name?"

"Carrie…just plain Carrie."

"And I am just plain Patience. In this house there are no niggers and most days only Mandy and I dine together. We would love to have company. During the meal Patience said, "I hope thee does not mind me saying, thy accent seems a mixture of Kentucky and… Georgia?"

"You got some good ears, ma'am."

"Thee is not dressed like a runaway. I suppose thee stopped at another Underground Railroad station near here and freshened."

"I was thinking the same thing," said Mandy as though she were an equal.

"This is a strange place," said Carrie. "It ain't like I thought it would be."

"We are who we are," said Patience. "And thee is not a runaway; am I correct?"

"No, ma'am I'm free as the breeze." Carrie reached into her bodice and retrieved a free paper. "See, Mr. Orlando Ficklin, gave me this signed and sealed from Judge Clark."

Patience looked over it quickly, folded it neatly. "I can see you keep this in a safe place."

Carrie wiped her mouth with the napkin, smiled. "Second safest known to woman."

Both Patience and Mandy noticed that there was something familiar about her smile. They looked at each other briefly, neither placing where they had seen such a smile.

"Tell me, friend," said Patience. "How came thee to this place?"

"When I was a slave in Georgia my mama told me back in '32 she happened up on one of my daddy's sisters who lived in a place called Waynesville. Once I got off the boat in Cincinnati I took a colored man's stagecoach called the Lion and the Lamb. That driver say it's a number of places I could go but if it was him he'd 'follow the money' and sent me here. I figured rich white folk think they know everythin' and if you didn't know colored folks' business, at least one of your servants might know my auntie. Her mama called her Oseye but her daddy called her Sarah."

"Sarah?" said Patience and Mandy simultaneously.

"Yes, ma'am," said Carrie to Patience. "I didn't tell Miss Mandy because from what I seen in Illinois, and since I got off that stinkin' big boat, most Yankees like runaways more'n they like free niggers. No matter what, I got me a good meal out of the stop."

"I ain't no Yankee!" said Mandy. "I'm colored just like you. And Patience told you don't use that word here."

"I'll handle this, Mandy." Mandy stood and began clearing the dishes. "Carrie, thy Aunt Sarah was with me in Georgia. She lives nearby. The two of us should go and see her post haste. If indeed she is the Sarah in question, she will be delighted to see you."

◊◊◊◊◊◊

Patience walked with Carrie over to Sarah and Charles' Ferguson's house where she knocked twice and walked inside without waiting for a greeting. The family was just about to enjoy a steaming plate of sweet potato cobbler.

Sarah looked up. "We knew from the knock it was thee, Patience."

"Yes, and look who the Lion and the Lamb just delivered to my door."

Charles had stood at the visitors' entry. "Do we know thee, friend?"

"No, master, we ain't met," said Carrie.

"I am no master," said Charles.

"I am Sarah Ferguson, dear. Who might thee be?"

"I am Carrie. It says Smith on my slave paper, but I ain't got me no last name yet, and reckon I'm free to change it to suit me." In another voice entirely she said, "Mama's name was Eve. She said my daddy was Esi and Kenneth's son Robin, and my auntie's name was Oseye, but she call herself Sarah. Mama said she look almost like my Grandma Essie spit her and my daddy out at the same time."

Sarah placed her hands over her mouth in wonder. After several seconds she opened her arms and Carrie ran to her. They embraced each other until Sarah leaned back and said, "That was quite a mouthful for a ghost."

"I ain't no ghost!"

"No dear, thee is not, but, but…here I am searching for words. It is so unlike me."

Charles came to her rescue, "My wife is trying to say thee said so much on greeting that it was unsettling."

"Many words for a long travel. Two months ago I'd never been to the next plantation without somebody guardin' me and I been practicin' them words in Georgia and Louisiana and Kentucky and Illinois and on the riverboat and here in Ohio…near about all my life. And here I am. Done traveled 9000 miles! I had to make myself do what was scary as walkin' up on a patroller's picnic, but here I am."

"Thee did well," said Sarah. "Please join us at table."

"We just et," said Carrie. But she spied the stuff of legend on the table. "Is that sweet potato cobbler?"

"Yes," said Sarah.

"Mama said Grandma Esi's sweet potato cobbler won the county prize for pies and cakes so many times they made her either quit or cook somethin' else."

Her young cousins five-year old Eva and the three year-old twins, William and Henry, had never heard that story. Carrie joined the family for dessert. After a few bites she said, "This taste like Heaven must." People laughed with her.

"Was the driver on the stage coach by any chance tall dark and handsome?" said Sarah.

"No ma'am. He was medium, honey brown like me, but ugly as sin. Why you ask? You seem to me to be married with chillen."

Sarah was taken aback. "Your aunt is very married as these three young ones and their older sister, were she still at home, should illustrate," said Charles. "My *wife* asked because thy Uncle Dan owns the Lion and the Lamb. She was describing him."

"Dan seldom drives these days," said Sarah who had found her tongue. "But would it have not been a special treat if your paths had crossed by chance?"

"Chance is a dance with no feet," said Carrie.

They retired to the great room that was a combination parlor and work room for Sarah.

◊◊◊◊◊◊

"Tell us thy story, niece," said Sarah. "Bring us up to 1847."

"I'm a maid; I ain't no storyteller."

"My father and brothers spent months at sea," said Patience. "Those who could not read had nothing but their stories to pass the time."

"I ain't seen no sea," said Carrie. "My story ain't much of one."

"Let us be the judge," said Sarah. "We all have stories and they are all worth hearing. That's what makes history."

"Master said we ain't got no history."

"Thy master was a liar," said Patience.

"You get no argument from me, ma'am. I'll give it a go." Carrie closed her eyes until she was sure of the order that she would follow.

"Mama was among the last slaves brought to a plantation in Virginia to the Jefferson place called Poplar Forest. That's where I was born. Mama said when the master died us'n got sold. My brother stayed in Virginia. The rest of us ended up in South Carolina til me and Mama got sold to Louisville, Georgia and then on to Statham. That's where we was when she run into you."

"Yes, she did," said Sarah. "How long did you two stay there?"

"Mama's buried there now. She died of the cholera sickness not long after you left us."

"If that was in the same year that we were there," said Patience, "your father died that year too."

"I was afeared that may be true," said Carrie. "Can y'all tell me 'bout him. Did he really look like you? Mama said he had freckles like yours, but she made him seem much taller, like that Lincoln lawyer."

"I don't know Lincoln, but all things in their time, Carrie," said Sarah. "Please continue thy story."

"You promise you'll tell me 'bout my daddy, ma'am?"

"Thee may call me 'Aunt Sarah'. I am a Quaker. We are taught our word must be good at all times, without swearings, pledges or promises. Yes, I will tell thee about thy freckle-faced father who was much taller than I." Sarah smiled and Carrie thought she was seeing her own in a mirror.

"Well 'long about '40, my Georgia master took me to the Metarie Race Track down in New Orleans and lost me and two others in a bet."

"Does thee mean a man bet thy life?" said Charles.

"I ain't thought of it like that. I ain't dead, though I miss them good people I was livin' with in Georgia. I guess that makes a part of me dead. Me, Joe and Suzy moved up to Kentucky to live with a good number of Master Matson's slaves half the time on the plantation in Kentucky and half the time on his place in Illinois. The rest of his slaves stay in Kentucky all the time, workin' them fields under his li'l brother and the other overseer."

"How could slaves have been in Illinois?" said Patience. "It is a free state."

"That's how I got here. Is that enough pay for me to hear 'bout my daddy?"

"No," said Sarah. "I am not trying to be mean, but I intend to tell thee a full story in exchange for a full story. The more you pay up front the more I'll deliver on the other end."

Carrie smiled. "Fair is fair. I'll be fuller than Suzy was before she had them triplets." She laughed and the others joined her. "So we be up in Illinois and this good white doctor called me over and asked me if I was a slave. I said, 'Sir is fat meat greasy?'"

"What does that mean?" said Patience.

"It means 'yes'," said Charles who as a white man married illegally to a black woman did his best to learn his wife's culture.

"At the time, I wasn't in the best of my minds. Master had slapped me three or four times like I was a child that mornin'. Then he sent me to fetch the doctor for him 'cause he had a stomachache. If I hadn't been a slave I would've slapped the scrawny cur into the next world."

"Why did he lay his hands on you?" said Sarah.

"Aunt Sarah, Mama said her first master slapped you and you was just a child!"

"So that story circulated?" said Sarah embarrassed at the memory.

"No man should lay a hand on thee," said Charles.

"If he learned that good lesson, it was after I left. He slapped me 'cause I had cooked his chicken the night before, and he convinced hisself that's what made him sick all night long. I wasn't tryin' to poison him. He should've at least let me have some of it instead of makin' sure all I had was the same fatback the others et. Before he et, he had the nerve to count off each piece right in my face! Even so, it probably was the chicken that made him sick. It sure wasn't my plan."

"Returning to the doctor, how did thee feel when he asked about thy condition?" said Patience.

"I wasn't in a condition. I was in slavery. But when he said Illinois law had made me free, I felt so good, he got jittery and said it wasn't that easy. He told me to keep quiet til he figured somethin' out. I thought 'bout his words and was addled. It had never entered my mind that there was a law that included n—" she caught herself, "colored folk.

"I went back to Master's place and I told Jane Bryant, my bestest friend among Master Matson's slaves. I knew Jane been looking' to run for the longest, but her husband already had free papers, though he worked for Master Matson like we did. The li'l coward was happy with things just so. Ain't that a mess, wife and four chillen all slaves and the daddy free?" The rhetorical question went unanswered. "For a week or so, if I saw Jane and wasn't no witnesses 'round, I said, 'We supposed to be free. Illinois law say ain't no slaves allowed'."

"What happened next?" asked Patience.

"Jane up and run with the chillen, but master's dogs caught her in just a li'l while."

"She should have simply sued," said Patience.

"Sued?" asked Sarah. "Free or not, even here in Ohio a black person cannot testify against whites."

"I forgot and have gotten ahead of myself," said Patience.

"Thee is ahead of most people," said Charles.

"That is why we love thee," said Sarah. She turned to her niece. "Then what, Carrie?"

"That good doctor, and the man who owned the hotel, took Master Matson to court to get them Bryants free. As for the rest of us, 'cause we didn't run they acted like we wasn't in the world. One day I fixed dinner and Master had this tall lawyer named Abraham Lincoln over. Made me cook a pheasant and a almond pound cake.

I used to think Master could eat, but Lawyer Lincoln put him to shame. My lips was waitin' for some of that cake but I waited in vain.

"Lawyer Lincoln and another man got hired to say Jane and her chillen wasn't even slaves. I thought for sure their goose was cooked. White folk look up to tall men like they seein' God. Later I heard the doctor and his friend, Mr. Ashmore, the hotel man, asked that Lincoln man to represent Jane and the kids. When they asked him they didn't know he was already fixin' to argue against colored folk bein' free. They even offered more money, but he said folk called him 'Honest Abe' and he had to do right by Master Matson and his partner."

"Why weren't you included in the case with Jane?" said Patience.

"'cause, like I told you, Jane had the nerve to run without even tellin' me. Course she was livin' in the slave house and I was in the big house. She claim later on, the night she made up her mind to run, she was afraid to go into the house and tell me they was runnin'."

"It sounds plausible," said Sarah.

"For the longest it sounded made up to me," said Carrie. "Anyway, Mr. Orlando Ficklin spanked that Lincoln and his partner Linder good and quick. Jane and her kids got their free papers. As for the rest of us..." her voice trailed off.

"But did they not figure that the rest of you were also being held as slaves?" asked Charles.

"Uncle Charles, you is my uncle ain't you?"

"Yes."

"No disrespect, but who can tell what white folks can figure? In my eyes y'all's some of the dumbest people God put on this earth. All slaves everywhere *should* be free. I guess that judge say to hisself, five darkies in this courtroom. I'm going pretend ain't but five darkies in this state."

"Amazing logic," said Patience sarcastically.

"Master come home in a huff. He give each field hand a dollar without tellin' 'em why. Then he stormed into the house threw one at me. I dodged but picked it up. Then he say, spittin' out his words, "Come here, Carrie, you puddin' head!" He grabbed my arm hard and said, "Do you swear on the Bible you didn't tell Jane to run?"

I wasn't scared of that bully and I knew ain't no way Jane told that it was me planted the freedom seed. I said, "Bring that Bible, Master. I'll swear on that one and four more."

"Then thee lied?" said Patience.

"Is fat meat greasy?" said Charles before laughing at his own witticism. "Justice is worth more than honesty, or even peace."

"I may have lied in a fashion, but I hadn't told her to run, when to run, or where to run. I just told her we wasn't allowed to be kept. And anyway, I didn't bear false witness against nobody. I know that much of the Bible. 'Do not bear false witness *against* thy neighbor.' I figured King Jesus knew the word 'lie' but he ain't said that. And if Master thought I was goin' get myself in hot water 'cause a fool was askin' me to jump in, he had another think comin'.'"

They all laughed.

"I still am not sure how thee was able to become free," said Sarah.

"Master and that slimy overseer Nelson was hurryin' me and the field hands still in his possession, back across the river before trouble start over us still bein' his slaves."

"Then he was kidnapping all of you," said Charles.

"If kidnap mean stealin' us, I'll give you that. Turned out he was *kidnappin'* six of the seven of us. That good lawyer, Mr. Ficklin stopped the lead wagon. He said, 'Sir, I could have you arrested for what you're about to do.' 'What you mean?' say Master. 'Jane say this young woman should also be free.' Master say, 'By the time you get a warrant I'll be on the other side.' Mr. Ficklin quick think and say, 'I will go with you and buy her there.' Master say, 'After you done cost me five prime pieces of poverty you want to ride beside me?' Mr. Ficklin say, 'As you know, slavery is not allowed in Illinois. I will ride the ferry with you and pay you good money as soon as we reach Kentucky."

"I like this Ficklin," said Patience. "He, the doctor, and the hotel owner seem to me to be true abolitionists, not merely men opposed to slavery. However, why did he not manumit the others?"

"Everyone does not have thy money," said Charles.

"Uncle Charles is right. Ten Kentucky slaves don't come cheap," said Carrie. "One way or the other, I ain't never seen no man good as Mr. Ficklin. I been thinkin' about callin' myself Ficklin if it's all right with you, Aunt Sarah."

"All God's children have the right to choose how they want to be called," said Sarah.

"Lawyer Ficklin bought me fair and square in front of a judge. Then I'm standin' there with that paper wantin' to hug it, thankful to God and Mama, and myself for all the prayers we done prayed for freedom. Then, I ain't goin' to lie, I got scared. I told Lawyer Ficklin I was scared to stay anywhere I done been. Like as not somebody would snatch me up all but in Illinois and there they overlooked me like I was a li'l ant in a great field. He asked if I had any people anywhere else. I told him I'd heard I had an auntie in a place called Waynesville, Ohio. He said he'd buy me a ticket to Cincinnati, tell me how to get to Waynesville from Cincinnati and give me some money.

"That was more 'ands' worth of gifts than I'd ever heard from a white man's lips but, like I said, I'd never been nowhere alone. I asked, nearly begged him, to go with me. He said even if he did we couldn't be in the same space on the boat. Besides, he had to get back to work. Before I got on that big boat he told me to stay down below with the other colored folk out of the light and never come up even if they gave us a l'il time for air. He did all that for me."

"The Lord is merciful," said Charles.

"That's the sure 'nough truth," said Carrie. "Now tell me about my daddy, Auntie."

"Before she does," said Patience," does thee have work?"

"I been figurin' I need a daddy worse than work. A colored woman can always find work. But who's goin' to shade me from all the world's mean people?"

"My cleaning lady has given me notice because she and her husband are about to have a baby. Mandy cannot possibly handle both positions. Would thee like her position?"

"Miss Patience, that would be a true joy."

Sarah said, "I have hesitated to say this but what is an aunt for if not protecting her kin? Carrie, you have much to learn. Even in the north a colored person is not free to speak her mind. We cannot do all the things that whites do. If thee listens, Mandy, can teach thee the invisible borders."

"You mean it's two different kinds of freedom, one for the white and one for the colored?"

"Something like that."

"And even among the whites," said Patience, "one for the man and one for the woman."

"This is the damnedest place! It seem like it's stealin' lives all through this place!" As the others remained painfully silent in contemplation of these hard truths, Carrie clapped her hands, refocused on the reason for her journey, and said, "'nough of my story. What 'bout my daddy? I heard you say he be dead, but I want a *full* story. Was he a better man than Jane's sorry husband? Did he ever ask 'bout me?"

CREDENTIALS

In the autumn of 1856 Thomas Hussey said, "Sarah, would thee like to help me manage my business."

I thought he was jesting but played along. "Shortly after you two were married, Patience wrote that she was training Emma. I would not supplant a wife."

Thomas blushed before saying, "Patience died too soon and owns too many businesses for any one not tutored in such affairs. My training is as a physician. Thee is a businesswoman."

The man was earnest. "Please, I am a simple seamstress with not enough business in a year to match a single thread of the commerce of any one of thy businesses."

He left me as though he were surprised. True my brother Dan had built a business and he had no formal education but he was ambitious to prove himself. I know and am content with myself. And yet, I brooded over the request. Common sense got the best of me and I came upon an answer that should have been immediate had vanity not gotten in the way. I suggested Thomas employ John Jolliffe a man his late wife trusted. True the ruling had gone against him in the Margaret "Peggy" Garner case, but the colored community was convinced American justice was a smoke screen for legalized oppression. None of us saw Jolliffe as a loser. We adored him.

Through my suggestion began a long and fruitful relationship between the two men. He did not prove Patience's equal but he successfully weathered the economic downturn but that is for another time and place.

◊◊◊◊◊◊

Less than a year later came the painful Dred Scott decision. I took the Supreme Court's words personally when they declared that I and my people are "beings of an inferior order, and altogether unfit to associate with the white race, either in social or political relations; and so far inferior, that they had no rights which the white man was bound to respect."

"Then despite a lack of binding thee still respects me?" I asked my husband.

Charles saw my wet eyes and heard me choke on the word 'still'.

He said, "I am bound by the Light not the dispensers of darkness." He crossed the room and my children watched closely as their white father embraced their black mother.

◊◊◊◊◊◊

One man is not enough to chase disdain. Thomas learned of my despondency and called for an abolitionist conference in Middletown at Patience Starbuck College, the integrated place of learning named after his late wife.

The main speakers were announced as John Jolliffe and Lucy Stone. Patience would have loved Thomas's moxie. No two people were more controversial or committed to The Cause in southern Ohio. The addition of my brother Luther and nephew Diego Perez to the roster of orators fanned resistance even more. I was looking forward to the gathering until together Thomas and his second wife Emma came to me and asked if I would be among the twelve who addressed the assembly.

I said, "I have never addressed any public body. It would be unseemly."

"Thee teases," said Thomas.

"I do not!"

"But thy whole life has been about sewing a better world," said Emma.

I turned to her and said, "Now it is *thee* who teases."

They could not convince me to speak but I did agree to attend and organize the meals.

"I cannot come with thee," my husband said a few nights before we were scheduled to leave.

"And why not?"

"I had prayed that thee would see it first and prevent me from having to say what is clear."

I was angry. "Now I am dense!"

"Please, there is sufficient stress in these times without it entering our bedroom." If this was supposed to calm me, the gesture failed. "Our marriage is not sanctioned by the state and my white shadow might cast a pall on thy good reputation."

I would not even allow Charles to hold me that night. Yet there was nothing I needed more. The next morning I deliberated further and remained unconvinced until Thomas reported that the county sheriff had declined to attend when told he could not bring arms to a Quaker campus. He had claimed that putting himself and his men at risk by being unarmed would be more foolish than anything he had ever done in his life.

My father-in-law, Clark Ferguson, stepped forward to recruit Quakers from throughout the Miami Valley to serve as buffers should there be trouble.

My husband came in for a short break from the fields as I sat sewing my last assignment before leaving for the conference. He touched my neck with hands so clean I could feel the moisture from the water basin he kept in the barn. Before his traditional kiss I said, "Thee is a riot on my reason."

Perhaps he had believed I was still upset. I stood and we kissed. On separation I said, "I understand and will go tomorrow alone."

"So long as I have breath thee will never be 'alone'."

◊◊◊◊◊◊

The conference was held in a hall named after Elias Hicks, the abolitionist who had most influenced Patience. Less than two hundred people were present, split almost in half blacks and whites. On the first day Lucy Stone spoke, followed by two local white men, my brother Luther and a white man from nearby Germantown. Jolliffe and Diego were among the second and final morning's speakers. The closing session occurred after the midday meal had been served. I had worked more than my share and everything had progressed smoothly. My sister-in-law Elizabeth said to me, "I and the others can handle the cleaning. Thee should listen to the culminating speeches."

I learned later that Elizabeth was in collusion with Thomas. Following what was billed as the penultimate speech from "a surprise guest," without notifying the others about a schedule change, Thomas Hussey, saw me seated in the rear and called out. "Friend, Sarah Ferguson, would thee care to have a word before the final speaker?"

Aside from Lucy Stone, no other woman had spoken and here was a colored woman being summoned to the podium in the place that was expected to be filled with an important personage. I have never been known to be cowardly and certainly was not so inclined with a roomful of witnesses who could soil my name. Low buzzing came from several sections of the room as I advanced to the front.

"I am not prepared, but—"

"Who are you that we should listen to you?" said a red-faced prominent white man associated with the Underground Railroad.

"Yes," said another almost hissing.

"That Friend speaks my mind!" said a third.

Without lowering my head I advanced to the podium in Quaker gray and white bonnet—though I concede at home I daily dressed differently. Likely knowing little of Quakers in general and even less of colored ones, did these louts believe I was a demure, docile, dark, dolt?

On arrival I used the power of silence and stern eyes to address the critics. Meanwhile I considered what to say that would give me sufficient credibility for those who counted. Should I state that I am a black woman married to a white man? An escaped slave? One selected by the proprietor of the college and presider of this gathering? That my mother's grandmother was the Queen Mother of Fante-land?

I honored myself instead of the questioners. "I am a mother of four and a wife whose chosen profession is seamstress. Should you be unaware, *labor omnia vincit*. Should *your* Latin fail you, the translation is, 'hard work conquers all.' Should that prove unacceptable for those who sit in judgment, know that I have labored both as a slave and as a free woman. I may not have the right to vote for the President of the United States but I have every right to testify before this august assembly."

Emma and other women led the applause that carried the day. Midway through my impromptu speech there was a commotion at the rear of the hall.

Pushing his way past four Quakers trying to prevent unwelcome egress, was a small mob of slave supporters led by Clement Vallandigham, editor of the *Dayton Empire*. The knee of one of the Quakers was bleeding from where he had been knocked to the earth, and my father-in-law had a wound on his arm from the thug's blow.

"What in Hell's name do you think you're doing here!" said Vallandingham waving a club.

"Minding our own business and you intruders?" said Thomas.

"Intruders? I know who you are, an outside agitator who has only recently come to Ohio, Hussey," said Vallandingham drawing out the surname. "You were married to the famous nigger lover who had the arrogance to name a school after herself and let niggers attend as though they are human. Why you are such a Hussey that your own wife would not take your name."

"Enough!" said Luther coming to Thomas's side.

Vallandingham flushed red. "I will not have a nigger address me as though I were a slave."

"Shut up, man!" said Luther. "Our presider is a Quaker as are these men trying to civilize you barbarians. I am not a pacifist. Were you each carrying two clubs, alone I would dismantle your posteriors. But I am with friends ready to become warriors."

"Show me your free p—"

"Do you understand the words 'shut up!' The remains of six club carrying race haters in this room will likely be mopped up if you do not depart post haste."

By this time Diego, Jerry Riley and several other men *and* women were on their feet and shouting threats and waving their fists.

"Please, gentlemen!" said Thomas nearly screaming. He need not have worried, Vallandingham and his minions were already exiting.

When order was restored Thomas calmly said, "We shall pretend that nothing untoward has occurred and move on to our final speaker." "We are blessed with the presence of no less than the governor of the great state of Ohio, Salmon P. Chase."

There had been no advertisement that Chase would be present. He was so despised in his hometown of Cincinnati that despite a successful campaign for governor, the bully boys had seen to it the illustrious man could not carry southern Ohio. A physical attack so near Cincinnati on a man with Presidential aspirations might prove disastrous.

I said, "Excuse me, Thomas, I had yet to complete my speech."

Thomas waved for Chase to remain behind the curtain and took his seat.

I said, "In conclusion, *pacem in terris*, or 'peace on earth,' will only come when we, the downtrodden, demand it. As for me and my house, we shall not be moved."

When the standing ovation ended I said, "I yield the floor to the great champion and governor of Ohio, Salmon Chase."

About the Author

Author Historical Fiction Series, Esi Was My Mother (1795-1861), Sarah's Song (2013), Out of the Shadow of Darkness (2013), The Courtship of Queens (2014), The Cloud's Whisper (2016), River Woman Joined at the Heart (2017), Modern Psalms in Search of Peace and Justice (2017), A Half- Moon Shining: Haiku from an African- American/ Quaker Perspective (1999), Summer Excursions: A Collection of Dwight L. Wilson's Haiku (2010), The Essence Of Haiku: The Relevancy of the Haiku Masters (2010).

Acknowledgements

Running Wild Press publishes stories that cross genres with great stories and writing. Our team consists of:

Lisa Diane Kastner, Co-Founder and Executive Editor
Jade Leone Blackwater, Co-Founder and Executive Editor
Jenna Faccenda, Public Relations Manager
Rachael Angelo, Business Relationship Developer
Lizz McCullum-Nazario, Blog Afficionada
Jodie Longshaw, Blog Afficionada

Learn more about us and our stories at www.runningwildpress.com

Loved this story and want more? Follow us at
www.runningwildpress.com, www.facebook.com/runningwildpress,
on Twitter @lisadkastner @JadeBlackwater @RunWildBooks

Previous Titles by Running Wild Press

Jersey Diner, Say You're Only For Me by Lisa Diane Kastner
Running Wild Anthology of Stories, Volume 1 with various authors
Magic Forgotten by Jack Hillman
Running Wild Novella Anthology with various authors
Running Wild Anthology of Stories, Volume 2 with various authors

9 781947 041073